BLACK OPS

CHRISTOPHER BRYAN

Diamond Press

Black Ops
Christopher Bryan

Printed in the Unites States of America
The Diamond Press
Proctors Hall Road
Sewanee, Tennessee

For more information about this book or the author, visit
www.christopherbryanonline.com

Edition ISBNs
Trade paperback: 978-0-9978496-1-5
e-book: 978-0-9978496-2-2

Library of Congress Cataloging-in-Publication data is available upon request.

First Edition 2017
Cover design by Kara Kosaka
Book interior by Elizabeth Beeton
Diamond Press logo by Richard Posan for 2 Ps
Photograph of Christopher Bryan by Wendy Bryan

This book is a work of fiction. Names, characters, places, and incidents either are products of the author's imagination or are used fictitiously.

In memoriam

Hoover

2000 – 2017

Faithful, loving, and beloved friend

Your love, O LORD, reaches to the heavens,
and your faithfulness to the clouds.
Your righteousness is like the strong mountains,
your justice like the great deep;
you save both man and beast, O LORD.
Ps. 36: 5-6

BLACK OPS

PROLOGUE

Sunday, 18th September, 2016
Colme Abbey in the county of Somerset.
The library, 10.11 a.m.

"I tell you," said George St John Aloysius Eliot, twenty-second Duke of Caernwick (pronounced "Cannick" by those in the know), "I saw the thing in Paddington Green Police Station on Wednesday... while they were showing me round. On some damned constable's desk! Amid all the glories of the new wing, which I was about to declare officially open... everybody bowing and grovelling... and there it was in plain sight... a cardboard folder with 'Bernard Standish' on it, plain as a bloody pikestaff."

George Frederick Aloysius Eliot, Earl of Arden, shook his head.

"Dad," he said, "you can't know for sure it was our Bernard Standish. There could be dozens of them."

"Bugger it, you still don't get it, do you? To start with, this was old stuff. If it were new it wouldn't have been in a cardboard folder, would it? It'd be in their computers. Someone had dug this out of records. And then, as I keep telling you if you'd listen, there was a post-it note stuck on it, 'Possible new information on 1986 hit and run.' Now are you trying to tell me there's likely to be more than one hit-and-run, investigated by the Metropolitan police, involving someone called Bernard Standish, and dating from 1986?"

"Dad, I still think you're over-reacting. It was thirty years ago, for God's sake. What serious new information could there possibly be in that file? And who could it have come from?"

"Well obviously, as I was there to be gracious and tell the world how bloody marvellous are the Metropolitan police and the new wing of Paddington Green Police Station (in that order), I couldn't exactly pick the damned thing up and start reading it, could I? So I don't know. But I'm concerned, and I think you should be."

The duke was still concerned that afternoon as he sat in his study. The boy was clever with figures and balances, which was good in the modern world, but he was too sanguine, too apt to assume he could talk or lawyer his way out of anything.

The duke shook his head. Not so! It was fortunate—indeed, as the late duchess, who was rather churchy, would have said, it was surely *providential*—that he'd glimpsed those documents last week. And it would surely be *criminal*—he smiled in spite of himself at his own choice of word—to ignore the gift.

And he still had his contacts, if he chose to use them.

ONE

Haldon Hill, near Exeter.
Wednesday, 21st September, 2016.
About 7.00 a.m.

"Damn dogs!"

Obviously they'd found something. They were barking like lunatics.

And now she could see them, higher up the hillside, rushing round in circles, leaping and cavorting through the undergrowth.

"Rufus! Lurcher! What the hell are you doing? Come here at once!"

But the two spaniels, who were normally if not exactly obedient at least willing to negotiate, were on this occasion not to be drawn.

Muttering imprecations, Jill Maitland turned from the road and started to climb, glad she had worn stout shoes.

"Now then," she said, scrambling through fern and dead branches, "what the devil are you two up to?"

She could see something on the ground. Something blue. Dark blue.

Was that what the two of them were barking at?

It had to be.

And now she could see it: a figure in a blue windcheater, lying on its side. Asleep? Unconscious? Dead?

"Hello there! Are you all right?"

Her call had no more effect than the dogs' barking.

She pushed aside low branches and now she was on top of it.

"Oh my God! Mr Soames!"

Mr Soames from the village, just down the road from her.

"Mr Soames are you all right?"

But even as she asked the question she knew Mr Soames was anything but all right.

He lay motionless, a small spider walking across his temple.

She bent and touched him. He was cold.

She felt for a pulse but his wrist was stiff and she could find nothing.

She reached into her jacket.

Thank goodness she'd brought her phone today. John was always on at her for going out in the woods with the dogs and no phone.

And thank goodness there was a decent signal up here. She touched in 999, her fingers trembling a little. She'd never called 999 before. Would it really work the way it was supposed to?

Actually, it did.

"Emergency. Which service?"

The voice was cool, impersonal, and for some reason that was rather reassuring.

"Er—police I think. Or maybe ambulance. I mean, I've found one of my neighbours lying out here on Haldon Hill. He's dead. I mean, I'm not a doctor or anything, but I'm pretty sure he's dead."

Two

Exeter. St. Mary's Rectory.
The same morning. 7.14 a.m.

"I see," said the Reverend Michael Aarons, Rector of St Mary's Church in Exeter, "that Oxford University has been officially ranked best in the world."

Detective Superintendent Cecilia Anna Maria Cavaliere, Exeter CID, floating deliciously between sleep and awake, reluctantly opened one eye (as if refusing to open the other could somehow keep at least part of her safely in the land of sleep) and looked up at him.

He was reading the BBC news from his I-pad.

"What?"

"It's the *Times Higher Education* world university rankings. Just published. Oxford's come top. So Oxford's officially best in the world! I bet Verity will be pleased."

Cecilia opened both eyes and considered how her friend and colleague Detective Inspector Verity Jones would react to this.

"*My* bet is she'll say, 'Everybody knows that.'"

Michael chuckled. "And if she's in a mood to imitate you, she'll add, 'at least, everybody who knows anything about anything!'"

"Hmmm," Cecilia said, and closed her eyes again.

She was just deciding that she really could float back into unconsciousness when there was buzzing and a sharp vibration from under her pillow.

"Damn! Now what is it?"

She sat up beside her husband, scrambling for the mobile phone as she did so.

"Detective Superintendent Cavaliere," she said to it when she found it.

"Sergeant Stillwell here ma'am. Sorry to bother you on your late morning, but somebody's gone and found a body. On Haldon Hill."

Haldon Hill — the old pet cemetery.

They found a *body*? In a *cemetery*?

"Are you having me on, sergeant? This isn't the first of April."

"No ma'am. The body's not actually *in* the cemetery. It's out by the Haldon Belvedere. DI Jones has gone out there with a couple from uniform, and Tom Foss is on his way to join them." Tom Foss was forensics. They were of course following normal police procedure in the United Kingdom when a cause of death was unknown. "It may just be the fellow keeled over. But DI Jones thought you'd want to be notified."

"Yes, sergeant, I would. Thank you."

She put the phone onto the bedside table.

"Does that mean you've got to go?" Michael said.

She looked round at the bed, which now felt more inviting than ever.

"I'm not going to rush. Verity's perfectly competent to assess the situation."

"But if it turns out there's been a murder?"

"Then I'll have to take charge. But maybe it won't be that."

Michael nodded.

There was tapping at the bedroom door, and giggling from beyond it.

"Papa, we're here! *Siamo qui, mama!*"

It was Rachel, their bi-lingual six-year-old, and her baby sister Rosina, whose small but distinctive English-Italian vocabulary already included such useful words and phrases as "breakfast" and "prima colazione".

Paws clattered on the parquet and a tail could be heard thumping against the furniture.

Evidently Figaro was also ready for the day to begin.

Michael shook his head.

"In the mean time," he said, "life goes on."

She nodded.

She wouldn't have had time for that extra sleep anyway.

THREE

Exeter. St. Mary's Rectory.
A little later that morning.

It was Michael's practice on what everyone referred to as Cecilia's "late morning" to leave the early Eucharist in church to Father Crane, a retired priest who'd once been rector of St. Olaf's in the city. So he and Cecilia were able to get Rachel and Rosina up, and take Figaro for a walk, and give Figaro, and Felix and Marlene (the cats) their breakfasts, and then have breakfast together with the children just as if they had been normal people instead of what Cecilia's landlady during her tour of duty in Edgestow had been in the habit of referring to as "an Italian lady policeman married to a vicar."

After a brief contretemps involving Rachel's desire to use her I-pad at the breakfast table ("Absolutely not." "But Susan Cole's mummy lets her do it." "At meals in this house, sweetheart, we pay attention to each other and to our food." "Oh."), they were all happily engaged in this pleasant exercise when Cecilia's phone buzzed again.

Cecilia sighed, and pulled it from the pocket of her jeans.

"I *thought* we weren't—" Rachel began, but then fell silent as her mother waved imperiously at her.

It was Verity Jones from the scene on Haldon Hill.

"Just to keep you in the loop, we *think* it's probably death by natural causes. ID was easy — the woman who found him knew who he was. Apparently he lived a couple of doors down from her in the village. Charles Soames was his name. Middle-aged bachelor. Schoolteacher. Taught maths at Alphington Grammar. Often walked out here for a constitutional in the early morning. It was probably a heart attack. That's what Tom Foss thinks. Of course he'll take a closer look before he signs off on it, but he doesn't see any reason not to move the body to the morgue. There's nothing to suggest this is a crime scene."

Cecilia nodded. "You've notified the station of all this?"

"Yes, ma'am."

"Next of kin?"

"The woman who found the body thinks there's an ex-wife. I passed that on, too. Someone's going to his house to see if they can find an address. Or anyone else to notify. Children, maybe."

Again Cecilia nodded.

"It looks as if you've got everything under control, Verity. Excellent."

"Thank you, ma'am."

"In which case," Cecilia said, looking round the kitchen at her family — husband, children, dog, cats — all gazing at her with varying degrees of curiosity, hope, and expectation, "those of us who are having our 'late morning' can return to our boiled eggs."

So she did.

But not for long.

About ten minutes later she was spreading marmalade on a piece of toast for Rachel when her mobile phone vibrated and buzzed for the third time that morning.

Rachel giggled.

Cecilia raised an eyebrow and picked up.

"Detective Sup — ."

"Glyn Davies here, Cecilia. I'm sorry to break in on your late morning. But I need you in my office. Let's make it 9.00 a.m. We have a situation."

FOUR

Cecilia arrived in the Heavitree Police Station car park just behind Verity. They got out of their cars together. Verity as usual looked immaculate and gorgeous despite having been on duty since six and rushing about the country since seven, and Cecilia as usual wondered how on earth she did it.

"Do you know what's up?" she said.

Verity shrugged and shook her head.

"All I know is, minutes after I'd called you, I had a call from the chief super saying he'd just been informed of Soames' death. I started to say we didn't think it was suspicious, but he stopped me in my tracks and said no, there were other factors I didn't know about, and as far as he was concerned it *was* a suspicious death. He was sending a murder investigation team, and we must treat the area as a crime scene until it arrived. He wanted forensics to be especially careful. I was to come in as soon as the MIT arrived and had been briefed, and he was sending for you and Joseph and the rest of the team."

"The team" was the Serious Crimes Team, which Cecilia headed, and Joseph, a civilian, was their Bahamian computer specialist—indeed, their computer genius—and also Verity's husband.

"So here I am," she concluded. "And that's all I know."

Cecilia shook her head. Such a direct overruling of an officer in the field was unlike Glyn Davies, but presumably they'd be learning his reasons soon enough.

They arrived at his office and were waved straight though by his secretary, to find Joseph already there, together with Detective Constables Headley Jarman and Tom Wilkins. The Chief Superintendent was not in uniform—the first time, so far as Cecilia could remember, that she'd ever seen him out of uniform in his office. He was standing by his desk wearing jeans, trainers, an open necked shirt, and a tough-looking waterproof jacket that appeared vaguely ex-army.

Actually, she thought he looked rather good.

"You'll be wondering what this is about," he said. "So pay attention while I fill you in. First, some history: in July 1986, something over a month before they were due to be commissioned at Sandhurst, a group of six officer cadets was approached by an operative of the Secret Intelligence Service and persuaded to carry out a black bag op on its behalf."

"Does the Secret Intelligence Service have authority over Sandhurst cadets, sir?" Joseph asked.

Glyn Davies shook his head. "It most certainly does not! I emphasize, the cadets were *persuaded*. To be frank, they were a bright and enthusiastic bunch, but still pretty wet behind the ears. The invitation played on their loyalty to Queen and Country as well as making them feel important at being involved in a real covert operation. Looking back, one realizes it was also an ideal setup from the point of view of the powers-that-be. If the operation was successful that was well and good. If it went pear-shaped and there were consequences—say, a civil charge—the cadets could be blamed or framed for high jinks or a prank. They could be dismissed from the service with little loss to the Army and none to the SIS. And of course they could be threatened with the Official Secrets Act if they tried to speak out. Perfect!"

Joseph nodded.

"Anyway, the cadets went for it. Officer Cadet Ian Salmon was to be in charge—Ian Salmon who's now Commander Salmon with the National Crime Agency. You met him a while back, Cavaliere."

He looked at Cecilia and she nodded. It was two or three years or so ago, but she recalled very well her meeting with Commander Salmon of the NCA—smooth, very smooth: tall, balding, quietly spoken, dark grey suit, Guards tie.

"What's a black bag op?" Verity said.

"Breaking and entering in the name of Her Majesty," Joseph said.

Davies smiled grimly.

"I think the official definition is something like 'covert entry by a government agency in order to obtain intelligence.'"

He paused—perhaps for effect? He was Welsh, after all, and had something of the bard in him.

"In this particular case," he continued, "the object of the break-in was a freelance journalist, a man called Standish. Bernard Standish. For some reason the security services believed he'd obtained information about something that was of concern to the government—and they wanted to see it. The team's job was to break into Standish's office, photograph whatever he appeared to working on at that moment, and then get out, without leaving a trace. Joseph, I see you shaking your head. Do you not approve?"

"It's not disapproval, sir. It's just that life was so hard back then. Nowadays all his stuff would be on his hard drive. Chances are he'd leave his computer turned on anyway. So all you'd need to do would be to stick a flash drive in the USB port. You could be in and out in two or three minutes. And that's assuming it couldn't be hacked from outside—and I dare say it could unless it was run through shielded cable."

The chief superintendent smiled.

"Yes Joseph, those were the days of wooden ships and iron men! Still, in the event it all went smoothly enough. They got their photographs and left, with no one the wiser, so far as they knew. Ian Salmon handed the photographs over to the intelligence services chap who'd asked for them, and that was the last he saw of him. The team all assumed the matter was over, and in the weeks leading up to the Sovereign's Parade—that's the Sandhurst passing out ceremony for those who are ignorant of such important matters—they were no doubt in a fair way to forgetting about it."

He paused again and drank from the mug of tea on his desk.

"But then," he said, "three weeks after the break-in, Bernard Standish was killed. It was a hit and run. A quiet street. No witnesses to speak of except his eight-year-old son. And no description of the car that was ever any use. The enquiry ran into the sand and the driver was never traced."

"Did that mean someone in the security services decided Standish knew too much?" Cecilia said.

Davies shrugged. "Enough to warrant what would, I think, be termed 'a special operation of a quasi-military nature'? I very much doubt it. Despite what you see in the James Bond films, British Intelligence doesn't generally go in for that sort of thing. We gather intelligence mostly either by persuading people that we're the good chaps so they really *ought* to talk to us, or more commonly, human nature being what it is, by persuading them that talking to us is in their best interest, which usually means we make it profitable. The point is, for British Intelligence to instigate someone's death it would have had to be something quite extraordinary. Believe me."

"So perhaps it was something extraordinary," Joseph said.

"Or else perhaps the whole thing was just a drunk driver and an accident," Verity said.

Cecilia nodded. There is such a thing as coincidence, and

human beings do love to see patterns and connections even when there aren't any.

"Agreed," Davies said. "It could have been just an accident. Still, the team was sufficiently disturbed to wonder whether Standish *had* been someone's target and whether one of them might be next. After all, if Standish's death was connected to knowing what was in those documents, they'd all seen them too."

"So what happened?"

"They agreed to take a precaution. If any of them felt threatened or endangered in a way that seemed connected to the break-in, they'd do their best to circulate a message to the entire group. It would consist of one word: 'catastrophe.' And that would be a warning to the rest."

"And so?" Cecilia said.

Glyn Davies shrugged.

"And so—nothing. For thirty years. Until the day before yesterday, when Andrew MacDonald, one of the team members, was in the Trossachs fishing on Loch Venachar. His boat was found drifting, with him dead in the bottom of it. Apparently he died of a heart attack. It looks like death by natural causes, and the Scottish police are treating it as that. I'm sure we'd have all assumed it *was* by natural causes: except for the fact that that same morning, MacDonald sent a text from his mobile phone. It consisted of one word. 'Catastrophe.'"

"But if that's on his phone, why are aren't the police treating his death as suspicious?"

"Because they don't have his phone. It wasn't with him in the boat, nor has it turned up anywhere else. My guess is it's at the bottom of Loch Venachar."

"So how do we know the text was sent?"

Davies picked up a phone from his desk, touched the screen, and showed it to them.

"Because it arrived," he said.

FIVE

Heavitree Police Station, Exeter.
Chief Superintendent Davies' office.
A minute or so later.

There was a moment of silence. Cecilia broke it.

"So *you* were part of Commander Salmon's team." She wasn't sure if it was a statement or a question.

"That's where he and I first met."

"So you've known him for a long time."

"I have."

"Forgive me, sir, but do you trust him?"

"I do. I don't mean I'm close to him or anything like that. No one is. He's a funny old thing, always has been. And he's shy—introvert with a capital 'I'—which he hides a lot of the time by being pompous. But he's also brilliant in an odd sort of way. And he has a sense of humour—in an odd sort of way. Above all, I'm sure he's a man of honour. A *good* man."

"And did he get the 'catastrophe' message the way you did?"

"He did. And he'd already contacted me about it yesterday afternoon—before we even knew what had happened to Andrew. But then—well, three things have happened since then."

They waited.

"First, there was a gas explosion in west London last night."

"I read about that on the BBC website this morning," Joseph said.

"What the BBC won't have told you, because it's under wraps, is that the explosion was in Ian's flat, minutes after he'd got back from work, and it surely wasn't an accident. It would certainly have killed him if he'd been inside. Fortunately for him he's a wily bird, and he has something set up so he can always tell if someone's been in his flat. So he ducked out—as he puts it, an eagle's talon ahead of the bang. He was quite badly injured—a broken arm and cracked ribs and a lot of bruises from flying masonry—but he's still very much alive and more than a little pissed off. Which if I know Ian Salmon at all bodes ill for someone."

"Maybe I was half-asleep when I read the report," Joseph said, "but I must admit I got the impression from it that the owner of the flat *had* been killed. Didn't it say they were looking in the wreckage for a body or something?"

Davies nodded. "That's the impression you were meant to get. Actually, if you look at the exact words of the press release, it's vague. Ian tells me there are already hints from a couple of sources we monitor that the word on the street is, the United Kingdom's had a senior law enforcement officer killed by terrorists and isn't willing to admit it. And that's exactly the word we want out there. Let whoever tried it think they pulled it off."

"So where is Commander Salmon now?" Cecilia asked.

"In a safe house with good medical facilities. I don't know where and I don't need to. We can get in touch with him when it's necessary."

She nodded. "So what was the second thing?"

He looked at her for a moment.

"Last night someone broke into our garage here in Exeter and planted a bomb under my car. Luckily for me, I was on the alert after Andrew MacDonald's message. So—I looked under the car before I got into it this morning, and spotted it. I called Ian Salmon, and he moved really fast: within less than thirty minutes a Western Power Distribution van arrived ostensibly to check the electricity meters, actually with two bomb disposal experts from Counter Terrorism who managed in what I think must have been record time to render the bomb harmless *and* create a controlled explosion in the garage that blew the windows out and, we hope, looked from the street as though the car bomb had done its job. Following which of course Counter Terrorism arrived without disguise, evacuated the street, and went through the motions they'd have gone through if it really had gone off."

He looked at his watch.

"I dare say they'll be allowing the residents back shortly. And I dare say there'll be the story of a gas explosion in Exeter on the news tonight—again, I think, with the hint of a fatality that we aren't admitting. And again, we're hoping whoever it was will think they pulled it off."

"What about Olwen and Arwen?"

"They're fine. And they've been moved to a safe house. Which again is what would probably have happened if the bomb *had* killed me. Olwen in particular was not amused at having to leave the house before she'd had her second cup of tea. Arwen, with the resilience of youth, seemed to take daddy being nearly blown up more or less in her stride."

"Same explosives as for Commander Salmon?"

"Not confirmed yet. But in any case it's hardly likely the two attempts aren't connected."

The phone on his desk beeped. He picked up.

"Yes, Joan."

Cecilia was near the desk and could hear the reply even over the handset.

"I've got Dr Foss on the line for you sir."

"Good. Put him through, will you?"

There was a click.

"Are you there, Tom?"

"I'm here."

"The Serious Crime Team is here in my office. I'm putting you on speakerphone so we can all hear you."

He pressed a button.

"All right, Tom, so what have you got?"

"You do understand this is all very preliminary."

"I do."

"Well, as you know, it looks like heart failure and that's what we all assumed initially that it was. Now there are several ways in which you can actually *induce* what appears to be death by heart failure—"

"The short version, Tom."

"Before he died, Charles Soames had been injected with something under the nail of the third finger of his right hand. Hardly the place you'd choose to inject yourself, and even with a fine needle it would hurt like hell."

"But has the advantage that a casual examination of the body might well overlook it?"

"Exactly. And I dare say we might have missed it if you hadn't alerted us to be on the lookout for something wrong."

"Go on."

"There's also a bruise on the back of his head, so I think the probability is he was knocked unconscious first, and then injected. At the site where his body was found, the MIT found no foot-prints belonging to him, but they did find two sets of prints belonging to someone else—one pair bigger than the other, maybe a man and a woman. The prints were quite well hidden—and then of course the woman and her dogs that found the body were wandering about up there too—so it was no wonder no one spotted them at first. But the prints are there all right. What's more, they're quite deep in places, as if whoever made then was carrying something heavy. There are also tyre marks on the grass verge at the bottom of the hill by the road — MOEs, so it looks like a Merc — where someone parked. We estimate time of death between eight and ten last night. So to sum it all up, it looks as if late yesterday evening a couple of people — the killers — rendered Soames unconscious, injected him with something lethal, brought the body from the village in a car, carried it up the hill from the road to where it was found, dumped it there, and then went back to their car. That's about it for the moment. When I've done an autopsy, I dare say I can give you some idea what the fellow was actually injected with. But in any case, I'd say it's certain you've got a murder on your hands."

When Foss's call finished, Davies looked at the others.

"That," he said, "was the third thing. There was a Charles Soames with us in the team for the black bag op." He looked at Verity. "As soon as I got in this morning and saw his name on your report, given what had happened already, I could hardly suppose it was a coincidence. That's why I sent the MIT and told you to treat the area as a crime scene. I was sure they'd find something criminal, and evidently they have."

Verity nodded.

"What I don't see," she said, "is if this has to do with a break-in nearly thirty years ago, why is it only happening now? What's just changed?"

"A good question, Verity. Ian Salmon and I asked it too. We don't know."

"May I ask, sir," Tom said, "did you get to see what was on the papers you were photographing? Do you know what they were about?"

"Yes and no. I mean, of course I *saw* the stuff I was photographing and so I formed an impression. It seemed to be mostly columns of figures, with arrows and lines here and there, and words written in. But I didn't make any effort to read it. I was mostly concerned with keeping the camera focused, and I couldn't for the life of me have told you what any of it meant. And of course that was just what *I* was looking at. We were all in different parts of the room, photographing different stuff. There were *lots* of papers. And we had no idea what was relevant and what wasn't, so we had to photograph it all. But there was no point in two of us photographing the same thing."

There was a pause.

"All right, sir," Cecilia said. "I think we get the picture. No pun intended. What do you need us to do?"

Glyn Davies gave a wan smile.

"I hate to say it, but poor Soames' death, as well as the attempt on me, has actually made that question easier to answer. You see, Ian Salmon and I have a problem. We trust each other but we don't know who else to trust."

Cecilia nodded. "It could be someone in the security services causing the mayhem, or it could even be a member of your team. It could be anyone who knew about the break-in, and you don't even know who did know about the break-in."

"Exactly. And all that 'could be' of course includes Ian and me. I may trust Ian. We may even trust each other. But *you* can't necessarily trust either of us. You see what a tangled web we're in."

He paused, and drank some more tea.

"Besides Ian Salmon, however, there's one group of people I do trust. And that's the people in this room. And now I have a reason to bring you into this affair, because whoever's behind it has conveniently given you a couple of crimes to investigate that are actually on your patch. And perhaps that's their first mistake, because you people are good. The best. I mean it. Maybe you don't hear that as often as you should."

He hesitated for a moment, then he said, "So, what I need all of you to do in the first place is simply your job: investigate this murder and work in whatever way you can with Counter Terrorism on the planting of the explosive device under my car. While you're doing that, I'm going to pursue something different, and I'm going under cover to do it — partly, of course, because if we want people to think I'm dead, I need to disappear. Ian Salmon's arranged for me to be excused from duties here. I'm to be seconded temporarily to National Crime Agency, and for all practical purposes to regard myself as working for the intelligence services."

"He can do that?"

"Actually, he can." He chuckled. "Let's say, there's more to Ian's connections and authority than meets the eye. Of course it's infuriated the Chief Constable *and* the Director of the NCA, apropos which Ian's comment was, 'if I can still rile both of them in a single day, then clearly my being spared last night has not been in vain.'"

"May we ask what you're trying to do undercover, Sir?"

"The first thing, at any rate, is there were two more members of the black ops team than we've so far accounted for. We need to check on them. Over the years they've gone off the radar. Ian's checking their last known whereabouts from his bed. There are one or two people in the NCA he's still sure he can trust, including a couple of researchers, so I dare say he'll come up with something."

"Can we know the names of these other black ops chaps, sir," Cecilia said, "in case they come up in what we're doing?"

"The names are George Patterson and Allan Brightman. And you've touched on something important. We need to pool our information as we go along. I've already told Joseph how you can keep in touch with me."

"And before you go you won't forget to collect those little gadgets I mentioned to you, will you sir?" Joseph said. "I think they could be useful."

"I won't forget, Joseph."

"Are you going under cover by yourself, sir?" Cecilia asked.

He smiled.

"Not exactly." He pressed the button on his desk phone. "Is Bob Coulter there yet, Joan?"

"He's been waiting for some time, sir."

"Good man! Send him in, please."

Sergeant Bob Coulter, a small man, stocky and grizzled, entered a few seconds later. He too was not in uniform. Cecilia didn't know him well, but was aware that when the armed response unit's services were needed, he headed it, and that Verity had a high opinion of him.

"Sergeant Coulter and I go back a long way," Davies said. "He's going to look out for me."

"But still just two of you?" Cecilia said.

The two exchanged a glance and Coulter smiled faintly.

"Coulter's tougher than he looks. Don't worry about us," Davies said.

At which moment, quite suddenly and without any warning, it occurred to her that a part of Glyn Davies was actually enjoying this. She didn't recall seeing him so animated for a long time.

But all she said was, "Fine! And the deal is, while we're busy not worrying about you, should we happen to get bored, we have our very own murder and our very own attempted murder to solve. Right?"

"Precisely, Detective Superintendent. You have it in one."

"Sergeant Coulter," Verity said quietly as they were leaving Glyn Davies' office.

"Ma'am?"

"I'm really glad you're watching the chief super's back. We're quite fond of him, really."

Bob Coulter met her eye and nodded.

"Copy that, ma'am," he said.

SIX

Exeter, Heavitree Police Station.
The office of the Serious Crime Team.
That afternoon.

Cecilia was with the Serious Crimes Team in her office.

"Now," she said, "while I think it's clear our murders and attempted murders are linked by a common purpose — eliminating members of the 1986 black ops team — they're obviously being worked by different people. One person, or one team, could have managed to plant a device in London yesterday afternoon and another here in Exeter last night. But they could hardly also have been killing Soames in Haldon and then taking his body out to the hill."

"We've also got two completely different MOs," Verity said.

"Exactly. So, as regards the planters of bombs, the Met have uniform doing door to door questions in the area round Commander Salmon's flat to see what, if anything, anyone may have seen or noticed, and I'm arranging for our uniform to do the same around the chief super's house. Let's see if between us we come up with anything."

"Presumably someone's also looking into the explosives

they used?" Tom said. "And what kind of bombs they were?"

Cecilia nodded.

"That's Counter Terrorism's thing," she said, "here and in London. We've got a whole bomb. They've got wreckage. As soon as between them they can tell us something, we'll know."

She paused.

"Now, as regards the other killers—the injectors of lethal drugs or whatever it was—that's really our thing. I want you two," she turned to Tom and Headley, "to go to Soames' house and really search it thoroughly. I know uniform have had a preliminary look, but see if you can find anything they've missed. Then ask around the village—the pub, the shops, whatever anyone may have noticed. It's a small place. Tom Foss says two people, probably a man a woman, were involved. Well, a couple of strangers are likely to have been noticed. See what you can get."

The two young detective constables looked at each other and nodded.

"Then after that," she said, "a visit to Alphington Grammar. See what you can pick up there. Was Charles Soames liked? Not liked? Whatever. You know the routine."

"No item is too small or trivial to merit our consideration!" Headley said.

"Exactly! To be a good detective is to be the archetypal snapper-up of unconsidered trifles!"

"Shakespeare?" Tom said cautiously.

Cecilia smiled. "Who else?"

"Well," Joseph said, looking up from his computer. "I think maybe I've just found you another unconsidered trifle."

"What's that?" she said.

"I've been checking Metropolitan police records and I've found at least *an* answer to Verity's question, 'What's just changed that's got something to do with what happened thirty years ago?'"

He pointed to his screen. "The file on Bernard Standish's death was updated on Tuesday last week, the 13th."

"Was it now?" Verity said. "That's very interesting. Do we know why?"

"His son Malcolm told the Met he'd found new evidence that he thought had a bearing on his father's death, and he'd like them to look at it."

"And what did they find?"

"They haven't looked at it yet."

"*What?*" Verity said. "And they had this a week ago? That's disgraceful!"

Joseph shook his head. "I think you're being a bit hard on them. They're trying to protect a city of 8.7 million people where the *normal* terrorist threat level is 'substantial.' I can quite see why a possibly accidental death thirty years ago might not be exactly top of their priorities."

Verity continued to look sceptical. Cecilia, who'd worked with the Met for some years, merely shrugged.

"Anyway," she said, "it can certainly be top of our priorities. I take it we have an address?"

"For Standish's son?"

"Yes."

"He lives in Paddington," Joseph said, and pointed to his computer screen. "Your old haunt, isn't it?"

"It is!" Cecilia said, looking over his shoulder. "Craven Hill Mews! I know exactly where that is."

She looked at Verity.

"Please don't say the game is afoot," Verity said.

"All right, I won't. Especially since Sherlock Holmes nicked it from *Henry V* anyway. But you're right, Joseph. It's a place to start. DI Jones, tomorrow morning you and I are going to Craven Hill Mews. Meanwhile, could you get Susan to let Paddington Green Police Station know we're coming and why? And with their permission while we're at it we might as well look at their files on the Standish thing. I suppose it's too much to hope the investigating officer is still around?"

Joseph shook his head. "No longer active. It was a fellow called Sterling. Detective Superintendent Sterling—with an "e" like the money, not the town in Scotland."

"Wait a minute," she said. "Greg Sterling? I remember him. He was still around when I was there. I didn't know him well—he was a lot senior to me. But so far as I recall he was nice, and a good copper. Everyone liked him and he had some good results."

"Well, he's retired now. But I can look and see if he's anywhere to be found."

Tom Foss phoned through later that afternoon. Verity and Joseph were in Cecilia's office, and she put him on the answerphone.

Clearly Dr Foss and his minions had wasted no time in examining Charles Soames' body.

"We found heightened levels of sodium chloride," he said, "as well as chlorine. Neither of these would normally rouse our suspicions, since both are found naturally in the human body. Given the circumstances, however, and the fact that your man appears to have been injected with *something*, our conclusion is that it was a lethal dose of potassium chloride. Too much potassium in the body leads to tachycardia—that's to say, a too fast heart rate—and that leads to ventricular fibrillation, which is one type of cardiac arrest. That's how your man was killed."

"It'd be an efficient murder weapon," Joseph said when Foss's call was ended. "Some American states use potassium chloride injections as part of their process for executing people."

"Good God!" Verity said. "That's utterly barbaric."

He shrugged. "And the form of capital punishment that wouldn't be barbaric would be—what? Hanging, perhaps? The electric chair? Maybe a firing squad? Beheading?" He paused for a moment and then added, "Anyway, quite aside from all my prejudices, I assume someone's now going to check very carefully on that fellow they found dead in his boat in Scotland? Given the circs, I'll be very surprised if they don't find he died in the same way."

Cecilia nodded.

"Yes Joseph," she said. "Quite aside from all your prejudices, point taken."

SEVEN

London E1. Chapman Street.
Thursday, 22nd September. 8:00 a.m.

Ian Salmon's being confined to a bed clearly had not impaired his ability to use his contacts — or at least those few left whom he was willing to trust. Within hours he had given Glyn Davies "last-known" addresses for the two remaining black bag team members. Both, as luck would have it, were in London, and not too far apart, which was convenient: George Patterson at an address in Cannon Street Road, and Allan Brightman in the gentrified part of Stepney.

They decided to visit Patterson first.

"I hate to admit it," Davies said as they stood in sunshine outside Shadwell DLR Station, "but this is starting to feel like old times."

"Except it's not so damned hot. And at least" — Coulter grinned reminiscently — "we don't look so bloody silly as we did that time we had to wear burkas."

"Oh, I don't know, Bob. I always thought you looked rather

charming. I was only telling Olwen the other day how much I fancied you in a burka!"

Coulter shook his head and chuckled.

"Still," Davies added, "we did manage to pull off a stunt that time — against a villain whose only weakness, as I recall, was a liking for country music."

"I'd hardly call that a weakness, sir. More like a fatal character flaw. All those wimpy blokes moaning about how their woman done them wrong."

Davies laughed. "Well, leaving aside your personal dislike of an art form that has given joy to millions, let's go and cause some more trouble, shall we?"

So they set off on the short walk to George Patterson's flat, which they found it easily enough: a pleasant little spot about halfway along Cannon Street Road.

No one answered the doorbell, though they rang twice.

Knocking got no response.

They looked at each other.

"Reasonable grounds?" Coulter said, peering at the front door. "This lock is a joke."

Davies shrugged. If one definite murder, one probable murder, and two attempted murders (so far) were not grounds for "reasonable suspicion" that a crime might be in progress, and so for entering without a warrant, he couldn't imagine what would be. And in any case, he reminded himself, they weren't at this moment working as police officers. They were working for the security services. Which meant they weren't there to gather evidence that they could present in court. They were there to obtain intelligence.

"Go for it," he said.

Coulter nodded, and within rather less time, Davies thought, than it would have taken him personally to undo the lock with the key, had picked it and was opening the front door.

"Bob, you amaze me," he said.

Bob Coulter grinned and muttered, "One more sign of a misspent youth!"

They entered without difficulty.

And they found George Patterson without difficulty, seated in an armchair in a pleasantly furnished sitting room in front of a silent, blank television. The television was silent and blank because it was one of those clever sets — indeed, the very latest and finest of its kind — that turn themselves off after an hour or so if no one pays them any attention. And no one had paid it any attention because Patterson himself was silent and blank: cold, stiff and extremely dead.

"He was injected under his finger nail," Coulter said, peering at his hand, "just like the other fellow."

Evidently their "suspicion" had been entirely "reasonable." They now had two murders on their hands. Definitely.

They could see no mobile phone. If Patterson received the 'catastrophe' message it had done him little good.

Davies sighed.

"Let's get out of here," he said, "there's still Brightman. We might be in time."

As they were walking away from the flat, he notified Ian Salmon of Patterson's death, and he said he would notify the Metropolitan police.

Brightman's address brought them to a handsome townhouse in Leadmore Terrace. A gleaming Alfa Romeo Giulia Quadrifoglio was parked in the road in front of it. The age identifier on the number plates indicated it was less than a year old.

"Looks like he's not short of a bob or two," Coulter muttered as they mounted the steps.

Allan Brightman himself answered the door. He was fatter than Glyn Davies remembered him, but otherwise entirely recognizable, and definitely alive.

For a moment he looked slightly disconcerted, and then —

"Glyn Davies!" he said, "My God, what a surprise! You haven't changed a bit! And you look well!"

"I am well," Davies said, "and I'm hoping to stay that way. But given events of the last few days that's not something I'm taking for granted. This is my colleague, Sergeant Robert Coulter. We're both with the Devon and Cornwall police — Exeter to be exact. May we come in?"

"Of course! Of course! Please do! May I offer you something?"

"Allan, we need to talk. Are you alone?"

"Audrey — my wife — she's out shopping and lunching with chums. Be back soon, I dare say! But I'm alone for the moment. Come up to my den."

Settled in Brightman's "den" on the second floor — a pleasantly appointed study, with a couple of nice oil paintings that Davies recognized as by Tina Morgan, a west country artist whom he particularly admired — he came straight to the point.

"Did you receive the 'catastrophe' message? On your phone? Or some other way?"

"The 'catastrophe' message? I'm sorry, old man, I'm afraid I don't know what you're talking about."

"After the black bag op we did at Sandhurst? We all agreed on it."

"The black bag op? Oh, *that*! — Well yes, I do vaguely remember — "

"*Vaguely*! For God's sake, Alan! The man we'd broken in on was killed a few weeks afterwards and we were all scared shitless."

Brightman nodded hastily. "Yes, yes, of course. That *was* a bit of a frightener, wasn't it! But Glyn, it was decades ago. Must be, oh, thirty years. What about it?"

Glyn Davies sighed. This was proving harder than he'd expected.

"Allan," he said, trying to be patient, "we were so scared we agreed to circulate a message if ever any of us felt threatened. One word. 'Catastrophe.'"

Brightman frowned. Then he nodded.

"That's right. We did. So what of it?"

"Andrew MacDonald—you remember Andrew MacDonald?"

Brightman nodded again.

"Andrew MacDonald sent that message on Monday. He texted it to me and to Ian Salmon. I take it you didn't get it?"

"Afraid not! Do you know why he sent it? Something scared him, I suppose."

"No doubt. What exactly it was, though, I don't know."

"So what happened?"

"What happened is that Andrew is *dead*. His boat was found drifting with him dead in it. He appeared to have died from a heart attack. *The same day as he sent the text.* Bit of a coincidence, don't you think?"

"Oh my God!"

"Exactly. And since then two more members of the team—Charlie Soames and George Patterson—have been murdered, and there have been attempts to kill Ian Salmon and me. So now do you get it, Allan? We've got targets on our backs—all of us."

"My God, that's terrible. I'd no idea. What should I do?"

"My advice would be, take some time off from whatever you normally do—what do you normally do, by the way?"

"I'm working in the City. Financial services."

"Well, take time off from it—make any excuse you like—tell your wife you have to go out of town—think of some reason, business, whatever—then get in your car, make sure you're not followed and go check into a hotel somewhere obscure. In other words make yourself scarce. And don't tell *anyone* where you've gone. Don't even decide yourself where you're going until you leave. That's what you should do, Allan."

EIGHT

West London.
The same day.

Cecilia and Verity caught an early train from Exeter to Paddington. It was a fine, bright morning, and after a cup of quite decent coffee and croissants in the station, the two women enjoyed their twenty-minutes-or-so walk over Bishop's Bridge and along the Harrow Road to the Paddington Green Police Station, where they were expected, and where Cecilia was greeted by several old friends.

It was evident that the Metropolitan Police were aware of the possible development in the Standish case, and had it on their to-do list. It was equally obvious, as Joseph had predicted, that with what they had on their hands from day to day, the thirty-year-old case was not exactly top of their priorities.

"It isn't just the terrorist threat level," a sergeant who'd at one time been a fellow PC with Cecilia told her. "It's all these bloody cuts. The government just seems to keep on wanting us to do more and more with less and less."

He was referring to current government economic policies that seemed to many to be eroding the nation's public services — most notably the police and health care. Cecilia nodded.

"I know," she said. "We've a lot of problems in the south-west, too. We're losing good officers."

The good news was that for whatever reasons, good or bad, the Met were entirely happy to have Cecilia and Verity take a look at the thirty-year-old Standish file, and investigate the possible new lead. They were given full access, and permission to make copies for their own files of anything they wished.

As far as the original file was concerned, that did not take long.

"There's not much here," Verity said. "This is barely a report. Why are there no witness statements? Surely someone must have seen something?"

"I don't know," the fresh-faced young constable who was assigned to assist them said. "I suppose so. But I agree this is pretty pathetic."

"I understand the investigating officer was Detective Superintendent Sterling," Cecilia said. "I used to know him slightly. I gather he's retired."

"Yes, ma'am. I know who you mean, but he was before my time, I'm afraid. I only started last year."

Cecilia nodded. "Do you think anyone here knows where he's living now? Maybe there are old friends of his? One of our colleagues is looking for his address, but this could save time. I'd like to hear Sterling's take on this, specially as the file is so thin."

"I'll ask around the older officers, ma'am."

Cecilia for her part promised to let the Met have a copy of her own report with whatever they learned after visiting Craven Hill Mews. These preliminaries completed, she and Verity went and had lunch in a pleasant little bistro, then walked back to Paddington Station, and thence toward Craven Hill Mews. As they were turning into Devonshire Terrace, Cecilia had a call on her mobile.

She continued walking as she answered it.

"Detective Superintendent Cavaliere here."

"PC Burns, ma'am, from Paddington Green. It was me that was helping you with the Standish file this morning. I've got an address and phone number for you for Detective Superintendent Sterling."

Cecilia exchanged a glance with Verity and stopped walking.

"Well done, constable!"

"It wasn't hard, ma'am. I just asked around. He's a widower you know. His wife died a couple of years back. Well now it turns out he's living with his married daughter and her family in Queen's Park. A couple of our blokes are long-time mates of his and go over to his daughter's place regular and have supper and cards or watch a match in the evening with him."

"Well, hard or not, this is very helpful. Verity, can you take this down?"

Verity nodded, produced notebook and pen, and wrote down a telephone number and an address in Queen's Park.

"Good," Cecilia said, looking at it after thanking the constable and ending the call, "Kingswood Avenue. I know exactly where that is. When we're done in Craven Hill Mews we can walk back to Paddington and catch the tube."

NINE

Haldon Village, near Exeter.
The same day.

Charles Soames' home was still out of bounds to any except the police. Crime scene tapes cordoned off both house and garden, and there was a uniformed constable at the door. Headley Jarman and Tom Wilkins were able to admit themselves and conduct their search without difficulty.

It was all rather depressing.

Surrounding them were the little things of a man's life... several photographs of a woman he'd obviously been fond of — perhaps his ex-wife? ...a diary in which he'd been writing about how he could see the sunset from his window... a battered volume of Tennyson's poetry by the bed, evidently much read. There were notes on his desk of things he planned to do in the garden, and some things he needed to buy for it. There was a grocery-shopping list, with a couple of exclamation marks beside "soda." A bookcase in his study contained a lot of books on mathematics and also quite a lot of poetry... collected works... Keats... Wordsworth... Browning... novels by Trollope... all of them looking well read. Obviously, Soames liked the Victorians.

There were medications on his bedside table. Headley looked at them.

"Even if Tom Foss hadn't spotted that Soames was murdered, I think these prescriptions might have made us wonder about him dying of a heart attack," he said.

Tom looked at him inquiringly.

"He's obviously under a physician. He's been prescribed atorvastatin 20 milligrams once a day, losartan-hctz 25 milligrams once a day, and a low strength aspirin. Those are what you prescribe for someone with some tendency to high blood pressure and high cholesterol. But if he'd had a serious heart problem there'd most likely be an anticoagulant instead of the aspirin."

"Isn't aspirin an anticoagulant?"

"It's an antiplatelet agent, which certainly helps prevent heart attacks – it stops blood clots forming. But for a serious heart problem you'd be prescribed a blood thinner like heparin or warfarin. In which case I'm pretty sure you *wouldn't* normally be prescribed aspirin as well."

Tom nodded. "Got it."

On the desk in Soames' study there was an open MacBook Pro. Tom touched the space bar and immediately the screen lit up. They peered at it together. There was a half-completed email to a woman called "Enid" – perhaps the woman in the photographs? His ex-wife? Or perhaps "Enid" was the reason his marriage had ended? Whatever, to judge by the opening paragraphs, which were all he had so far written – it was thanking her for a recipe she had just sent to him, and then talking about his birdfeeders and the approach of autumn – it seemed they were on affectionate terms though not passionate.

Headley watched as Tom scrolled down and there was the email from Enid herself, with the recipe – for a rich fruitcake – and then an account of visiting something called the Canoe Club with her friend Kara, where they'd turned themselves into pretzels in a yoga class and then floated around in the pool to recover.

"I think I'm starting to like Enid," Tom said as he read this through.

"And luckily," Headley said, "she's one of those people who put their full name and postal address at the end of their emails. Enid Soames. Klahanie Drive, Port Moody, British Columbia. She's in Canada. I think she was his ex-wife. I suppose it could be his sister."

"You know," Tom said, "looking at this, if she was his wife I'm not so sure she was ex. Maybe they were just separated."

Headley peered over his shoulder, read through the letter and nodded.

"I see what you mean. You're right. Anyway, we'd better take the computer with us. I imagine once it's turned off it'll need a password, but I dare say Joseph knows how to deal with that."

"Right."

He looked round.

All the little things of a man's life — brutally cut short in a moment of time.

At such moments he found it easy to detest the people they were trying to catch.

And in one way he didn't mind that.

"This job's much easier when you can hate the bad guys," he'd said to Detective Superintendent Cavaliere recently, after a man who tried to kill her turned out to be a man who also gave a lot to charity.

She laughed.

"It's a perk, but it isn't necessary," she said. And then she looked serious. "Actually it's quite dangerous. Human beings are scary creatures. None of us knows what we're capable of... good or bad. That's why we need order and law. Not just order... the Fascists promoted that. They got the trains to run on time. But they indulged in mass murder to do it."

She paused for a minute, then finally she said, "We've somehow got to balance people's right to decide for themselves how they want to lead their lives with structures that won't let them take that right away from other people."

After which observations it had occurred to Headley that Detective Superintendent Cavaliere was herself a somewhat scary creature.

Perhaps it came of being married to a vicar.

Regarding their present case, it seemed they were getting some feel for Charles Soames the man but not much to help them directly in solving his murder. There was nothing to connect him with break-ins, black ops, or any other nefarious activities, although a regimental flag over his desk and several photographs of him in uniform and with what looked to be old army buddies bore clear enough witness to his having served in the army.

"First Battalion The Devonshire and Dorset Regiment," Tom said from behind him, looking over his shoulder at the flag. "That was my granddad's lot in World War II. Very proud of them he was. '*Semper fidelis*,' he'd say. 'Always faithful' — that's what a man ought to be. That was their motto."

"'Was'?"

"They don't exist anymore — well, not as a separate regiment. The D&Ds were amalgamated in 2007, and the Colours were laid up in the cathedral. I'm glad granddad wasn't around to see it. He would *not* have been amused."

Headley nodded.

There was no mobile phone in the house — or at least none that they could find, though they looked hard — and no indication as to whether or not Charlie Soames had ever received the "catastrophe" message.

They left, frustrated.

Half an hour or so later, in a small general store half way along the next street, they had more luck.

"Let me see, when was it?" the man in shirtsleeves and a green overall behind the counter said, scratching his balding head. "Tuesday afternoon? Yes! That's right! Tuesday afternoon it would have been. Just before closing. I know that because Jimmy was busy starting to put up the blinds. Anyway, these two come in. Definitely not from round here they weren't. A man and a woman it was. Good looking, but foreign. Maybe Italian. They had funny accents, anyway."

Tom was smiling. No doubt he would enjoy telling Detective Superintendent Cavaliere about the funny accent that was probably Italian.

"What did they say?"

"They wanted to know where Haldon Crescent was."

"And you told them?"

"Well, yes. I mean, they was civil enough. And I'd no reason not to, had I?"

"Of course you hadn't. Thank you."

TEN

West London.
Later the same day.

"**N**ice!" Verity said, looking round the pleasant, cobbled street that was Craven Hill Mews. "And here's the house we want!"

They rang the bell, and after a few minutes a tousle headed man in jeans and an open-necked shirt appeared.

They produced their warrant cards.

"Good afternoon, sir. I am Detective Superintendent Cecilia Cavaliere of Exeter CID, and this is Detective Inspector Verity Jones, also Exeter CID. Are you Malcolm Standish?"

"I am."

"Mr Standish, you recently notified the Metropolitan Police of what you believed was new information regarding your father's death."

"I did."

"We're following up on that in co-operation with the Met because we think it may also have bearing on a death we're currently investigating in Exeter. Could we come in, please?"

"Certainly. I'm afraid it's a bit of a mess."

He led them into a pleasant enough room that was full of boxes and packing, with books and pictures on the floor. A woman was wrapping ornaments in sheets of tissue paper.

"This is my wife Julie," he said.

"I'm sorry I can't offer you anything," she said, "but as you see we're closing the place down, and there's nothing here to eat or drink! We're having to go to a café round the corner when we need to eat."

"That's quite all right," Cecilia said. "But we would grateful if you could take some time to tell us about this new information."

Julie looked at her husband.

"Well," he said, "my mum died in June, and she left us the house, which we're going to sell, because we don't want to live in the smoke. That's why we're packing everything up."

Cecilia nodded.

"I think," he said, "that what you want to know about is my dad's study, which mum had left pretty well untouched after he died. I mean, the cleaning lady went in and dusted it every week, but no one ever touched his papers or his post-it notes and things. So it was rather strange, really, trying to sort it out. There was a copy of *The Guardian* on his desk from the day he died—21st of July 1986—with an article about the likelihood of a company called Eurotunnel being formed to operate a proposed Channel Tunnel! I tell you it felt like entering a time warp."

Cecilia and Verity both nodded.

"But what I thought might have a bearing on my dad's death was some stuff I found in a legal pad in what he used to call his 'current work' drawer—which I think has to be connected to whatever was the last story he was working on. I thought the police would want to see it. Hang on, let me get it."

He went into the next room, and came back with a yellow legal pad that he laid on the table. The top first page was headed "COL GOV & CARTS" in somewhat untidy block capitals, underlined, and the rest of the sheet was filled with handwriting—notes, figures, quotations and occasional comments.

"My dad," he said, "was a bit of a Luddite about technology, at least as far as writing went. He used to say, all you need to be a good reporter is your eyes and ears and a notebook and a pencil. And, of course, dogged persistence."

Cecilia smiled. She rather thought Michael would have liked Bernard Standish.

"Even back then," he said, "most journalists were starting to use a word processor or something like that. But Dad reckoned he'd made his big concession to progress when he went from foolscap to A4—and I think he only did that because it was getting harder and harder to get the old sizes. Anyway, he used these pads to jot down notes of stuff he was collecting to use in his next article. As you can see, the first stuff in this pad is all about drug cartels and the government in Columbia, and he actually published that one. It was the last thing he did. But later on—well, look!"

He shuffled through yellow pages covered with writing until he came to a page headed "US AND I" in block capitals, underlined.

"There," he said. "What do you make of that? He was obviously on about something."

The two detectives peered down. Beneath the heading they were faced with columns of figures, marked here and there with pencil—a figure ringed, another marked with a question mark, another joined to another with an arrow. And there were various names—lots of names—written some in pencil, some in ballpoint. It certainly fitted with what the chief superintendent remembered seeing all those years ago.

"Can we look at the drawer it was in?"

"Certainly."

The drawer contained a dozen or so such yellow pads, evidently going back over several years, and all containing sets of notes in the same somewhat untidy hand, each with a sometimes enigmatic heading in underlined block capitals.

"As you see," he said, "dad's wasn't exactly the most elegant hand in the world, but it's all perfectly legible — except his abbreviations aren't always obvious. I dare say they were obvious enough to him."

Cecilia nodded.

"Don't you think the police will have looked at these pads at the time?" she said.

"I don't know what they looked at. I know they came to the house and I think I remember them looking in dad's study. But I don't know how thorough they were."

Again she nodded.

"Why are you so sure that what's here has a bearing on your father's death, Mr Standish?" Verity said.

"Well," he said, "I'm not actually *sure*. I think it might. I do know dad was an investigative journalist who was good at what he did and annoyed a lot of people. And because of where it was, as I said, I'm virtually certain this stuff has to do with the story he was working on when he died. His death stopped it being published. So if there was someone who didn't want that story published, his death was to their advantage, wasn't it?"

The two detectives looked at each other.

"I take your point," Cecilia said after a moment. "So much so, that I want to take this pad into evidence. I'd like to have it examined more closely. Of course we'll let you have it back."

"I understand," he said. "And don't worry about when it comes back. I'd just be grateful to know someone was going to take a proper look at it."

He hesitated.

"I was with him when it happened, you know. We'd been for a walk and an ice cream. I can see it as if it was yesterday. We were going back home and as we stepped off the pavement to cross the road for some reason—I'll never know why—dad seemed to jump forward. Then I felt a push from behind but as I started to fall forward someone grabbed me and pulled me back, or I suppose I'd be dead too. It was a man, I'm pretty sure. He covered my eyes—I suppose to shield me from seeing what happened. And then he walked me over to a seat in a bus shelter and sat me down and left me. And I never saw him again."

"And was he the only person there?"

"Oh, no, there were others. People were fussing round and saying 'poor little chap' and things like that from practically the first moment, and I remember the man saying 'keep an eye on him.' And then after a bit there were police and a woman police officer was very kind and took me home."

"So you never saw what actually happened? Not the car, or anything?"

"No. When the man let me look up I just saw people crowding round something in the road, and I didn't see my dad anywhere and then somehow I realized something awful had happened to him."

"And how old were you?"

"I was eight."

Cecilia shook her head. "Well, I'm sorry to have asked you to recall it all again. It must have been terrible."

"It was a long time ago." He sighed and looked at his wife. "But I still have nightmares about it sometimes."

ELEVEN

Exeter, Heavitree Police Station
Later the same day

Following Headley's and Tom's return from Haldon with their new information about Charles Soames' email correspondence with Enid Soames and the details of her Canadian address, Joseph promptly got in touch with the Port Moody Police Department. The timing could hardly have been better, for it was early afternoon in England, which meant that it was early morning in British Columbia.

His call completed, he came up from his office in the basement — what he sometimes referred to as "the Boffins' underground kingdom" and sometimes as "the room where we keep our *very* expensive toys" — and gave them the news.

"The Canadians were very helpful. They said they'd send officers this morning to talk to Enid Soames and break the news to her about her husband's death. And then they'll try to arrange for us to talk to her."

"Good," Headley said. "So as DI Jones isn't here to rebuke me for saying it, I'll dare to whisper very softly, *the game is afoot!*"

By way of completing their assignments from Detective Superintendent Cavaliere, the two young detectives then took themselves off to Alphington Grammar School, where their inquiries were rewarded with the information that Charles Soames was generally well liked and regarded by both his colleagues and his pupils, and that his death had cast a pall of gloom over the entire establishment. But they learned nothing that could be said to advance their investigation into the reason for his death.

Here, it seemed, there were no unconsidered trifles to be snatched.

TWELVE

North West London, Queen's Park.
The same day.

The house in Kingswood Avenue was good, solid Victorian brick, well kept with an immaculate garden, and facing the park.

A pleasant looking woman in her thirties answered the doorbell. When Cecilia produced their warrant cards and asked if they could talk to former Detective Superintendent Sterling, she smiled at once and said, "Of course! Come in! He's busy making his model boats, but he'll be pleased to see you. Come into the sitting room!" Then, obviously directing her call over her shoulder and up the stairs, "Dad! There's some of your old mates come to see you! I've put them in the sitting room." She turned back to Cecilia and Verity. "I'm Sherri Mason, his daughter. I've just made a pot of tea this very minute. Can I bring you a cup? All fresh!"

"Actually I'd love one!" Cecilia said.

"Me too."

They were settled comfortably in the sitting room, admiring a rather splendid model of the *Cutty Sark*, fully rigged (so far as Cecilia could see), when ex-Detective Superintendent Greg Sterling appeared, grey haired and cheerful, insisting that he'd like a cup of tea too.

She recalled him at once: a little plumper and greyer than he had been, but otherwise, so far as she could see, much the same man.

"I remember you!" he said. "You were PC Cavaliere, weren't you? I think you arrived in…" he hesitated, "round about Christmas 2000?"

"That's right," Cecilia said.

"'Course he remembers you," his daughter said as she served him his tea. "I remember what he said to mum the day you arrived. We were all having our supper together in the kitchen. 'You should see our new PC!' he said. 'She's got an Italian name and she's a right corker!'"

Her father actually blushed.

"I'm sure I never said anything of the sort!" he said, but Sherri only laughed, gathered the unneeded tea things, and left.

"Did you build that beautiful model?" Cecilia said when they had properly introduced or re-introduced themselves and were settled with their tea.

"The *Cutty Sark*? Most of it. Though Joe does a lot too—that's Sherri's husband. He's a teacher. And now little James and Ginny—that's their kids—are getting interested as well, so we're quite a crew. We're building the *Ark Royal* now."

"The aircraft carrier?" Verity said.

"No, no! The original *Ark Royal*—Howard's flagship against the Spanish Armada. I find modern ships boring to make. I like ships with *rigging*—and I'm afraid I'm giving the youngsters all of my prejudices!"

They laughed.

"Well, " he said, sitting back in his chair and laying aside his teacup, "you've come quite a long way today." Then, taking them by surprise, he continued, "And I suppose you're here about the Standish business?"

"Yes we are," Cecilia said, "but how did you know?"

"Oh, a couple of my old lads were over last week to watch the match and they told me. Standish's son has come forward with some new information and they thought the case might be reopened. So I half expected someone might come round. Mind you, I thought it'd be from the Met, not Exeter. As I say—you've come a long way!"

"We think the new evidence may bear on a case we're investigating in Exeter, so the Met's allowing us to have an early look at it."

"Well that's interesting," he said. "So how can I help?"

"We've been looking at the original file. There don't seem to have been many witnesses. In fact, frankly sir, there doesn't seem to be much in there at all."

"No, there isn't. It was a frustrating business from that point of view. We got the impression there'd been quite a few people about when it happened, but then damned if hardly anyone would come forward when we asked for witnesses. We couldn't even get a decent description of the car."

"What about the chap who pulled his son back and maybe saved his life?"

"Ah! You've been talking to Standish's son, haven't you?"

Cecilia nodded.

He shook his head.

"Well, he said that's what happened, and I'm sure he thought he was telling the truth, but damned if we could find anyone who said he'd pulled the lad back. And it's not as if it was anything to be ashamed of, is it? He was only a little fellow and he was upset and confused. How could he not be? So perhaps he fell back, and thought someone grabbed him. But it's a puzzle."

Again Cecilia nodded. "I suppose that's possible. More important—when we talked to him today he seems to think it possible the hit-and-run was deliberate—that his father was murdered for the story he was writing. Do you think that's possible?"

Sterling sighed. "I suppose he'd like to find some meaning in his father's death. Who can blame him for that?"

Cecilia raised an eyebrow. "I'm not sure I follow you, sir. Why would his father's being murdered give his death meaning?"

"If he was killed for the truth, for saying something that he thought needed to be said — wouldn't there be meaning in that?"

She nodded slowly. She supposed that might be true.

"Did you look at what Standish was working on, by any chance? In your original investigation?"

"I looked at his desk — at the notes and things."

"And?"

He shrugged. "It was notes. A man at work, but nothing finished."

Again Cecilia nodded. Personally, she thought he ought to have looked more closely at those legal pads, but she said nothing.

"Do *you* think there's any chance Mr Standish *was* murdered?" Verity asked.

He sighed. "There was certainly a hit and run. Which in any case is a criminal act. If we'd found who was responsible he'd almost certainly have gone to prison."

"But you don't actually think it was murder," Verity said.

He hesitated.

"No," he said finally, "I don't."

Yet he was surely uncomfortable about something?

There was a pause.

"May I ask," he said, "what's happened in Exeter that you think may be connected to what happened to Standish?"

Cecilia gazed at him for a moment. Normally she was rather careful when interviewing to make sure that she got information rather than gave it, but there were exceptions. On a hunch, she decided that this was the moment to make one.

"Yes you may," she said. "Three men have been murdered, one of them in Exeter, which is why we are involved. There have also been two attempted murders, one of them in Exeter, which only failed by good luck and some unusually sharp reactions by the potential victims. And all five of them, thirty years ago, had an opportunity to see whatever it was that Bernard Standish was working on when he died. And this burst of mayhem has all happened in the few days since Malcolm Standish said he had new evidence."

"Oh my God."

His expression told her at once far more than she had revealed. It told her that whatever Greg Sterling had known or guessed about the death of Bernard Standish, it was not this, and that he was appalled by it. Either that or he was an actor of unusual talent, which she doubted.

"So you see," she said, "this is what we need help with—all the help we can get."

He nodded.

"I wish to God I could help you," he said. "But I can't."

THIRTEEN

Somewhere on the Great Western Railway
between Paddington and Exeter.
Evening of the same day.

They were on the train going home.

"Do we need to go back to the station when we get to Exeter?" Verity asked. "Or can we go straight home?"

Cecilia, sitting opposite her, shook her head.

"Straight home," she said. "We can sort out what we've got tomorrow morning."

"Good. Only Joseph's by himself with Samuel."

"Ditto Michael with ours."

There were several minutes of silence.

Verity blew out her cheeks.

"We don't seem to have much, do we?" she said.

"Not a lot."

For several more minutes Cecilia watched her friend gazing out of the carriage window at passing fields, at their own faces dimly reflected in the glass, and the monotonous flicker of telegraph poles in failing light.

The rhythmic clatter of wheels on rails was quite hypnotic.

Verity's blonde head was nodding and her eyes were closing.
She's starting to doze off...

But then the blue eyes opened wide and —

"What do you make of him?" she said.

"Sterling?"

"Yes."

Cecilia sighed, and considered.

"I think," she said slowly, "that he's a decent man. That's
based not just on today but on everything I knew and heard about
him in the years while I was at Paddington. What's more, he was
obviously a damned good copper."

She stopped.

"Equally obviously," Verity said, "there's a 'but' coming."

Cecilia frowned and shook her head.

"Not exactly. Quite honestly, I'm confused. When we talked to
him this afternoon he was very clearly uncomfortable about
something — something about this case. But I'm not sure what."

"So you're not sure you believe him?"

"No, I'm not sure. And I mean that. I'm *not* sure." She paused.
"Look at his choice of words! When we asked him about the man
who pulled young Standish back from the road he was quite
blunt and straightforward. He was damned if they could find
anyone who'd admit to saving the lad's life! It was a puzzle!
But then when we asked him whether he thought Standish had
murdered, he twice avoided giving a direct answer. And then
when he did answer directly, it felt to me for all the world
like a man who really doesn't like to tell lies, but then sees no
alternative, so he bites the bullet and says what he must."

Verity nodded.

"But then," Cecilia continued, "when I told him what had
happened to cause our investigation in the first place — "

"Breaking your usual rule to get information and not give it!"

" — breaking my usual rule, as you say — well, I'm quite sure he really was stunned and horrified. And then when he said he wished to God he could help us, I believed him. But all that's just me doing a cold read of him. I don't have a thing you could call evidence to back up any of it."

There was a pause.

"I think," Verity said, "that in his original investigation he also made one very bad mistake."

Cecilia looked at her.

"He should have examined those legal pads more closely. To say, 'just notes' and leave it at that... it's not very thorough, is it?"

Cecilia sighed. She'd always liked Greg Sterling, and the more so after her chat with him this afternoon and seeing him with his daughter. But Verity was right. He'd surely made a bad mistake. And perhaps he knew it.

But Verity wasn't finished.

"On another tack," she said, "when we examine the pad, I really hope we can work out who 'Us and I' are. Was that going to be his title? Or was it something else altogether?"

Cecilia shook her head. For these questions too she had as yet no answer.

FOURTEEN

The Serious Crimes Team was gathered round the speaker phone in Cecilia's office. Glyn Davies and Bob Coulter were talking to them from London, and Ian Salmon from wherever he was. Over the last hour they had caught each other up on the previous day's developments and discoveries.

They began with a negative.

Uniformed officers questioning house-to-house and flat-to-flat in the areas near where the bombs had been planted had so far come up with nothing useful.

There were also, however, two positives.

One was that Scottish police, following the suggestion of their English colleagues, had arranged for an autopsy on the body of Andrew MacDonald, and the result was exactly as Joseph had foreseen. The medical examiner found evidence of his having been knocked unconscious, of an injection under the middle fingernail of his right hand, and heightened levels of sodium chloride and chlorine in the body.

"So," Davies said, "given it looks as though two sets of killers are being employed—one lot going in for explosives, and one for faked heart attacks—the heart attack specialists seem to have struck in Scotland, then come down to Devon, then gone to London."

"And while they were in Devon it looks as though they let themselves be seen by a witness in Haldon," Cecilia said. "We should get someone to him with photofit to see if we can get a picture of them."

She looked at Headley and Tom, who nodded.

"I see no harm in that," Salmon said, "though I doubt it'll get you far. These are professionals. They're unlikely to be on anyone's database. So anything you get on them—descriptions, even fingerprints, DNA—will almost certainly get you nowhere."

"'*Almost* certainly,'" Cecilia said, "isn't quite the same as 'certainly.'"

"Granted. I bow to your thoroughness, Detective Superintendent Cavaliere. Even more promising, perhaps, is that their being professionals means that someone is paying them, and I assure you they won't come cheap. So somewhere there must be a money trail."

Cecilia nodded. "Then we keep an eye out for that too."

The other new piece of information was from Commander Salmon. Anti-Terrorism and the National Crime Agency had done their analysis of the explosives used at his flat and in the chief superintendent's garage.

"Both," he told them, "were of the same type: a plastic explosive—PVV 5A. It was developed in the Soviet Union and is still manufactured in Russia. They use it, among other things, in antipersonnel mines. All of which in the first place confirms what was already quite evident, that the two explosions were connected. But also tells us something new, that those responsible for them are likely Russian, or have Russian connections."

"What could your people tell us about the device?" Coulter asked.

"Sophisticated," Salmon said, "obviously by people with military training — Russian military training, to be precise — which of course fits with the explosive."

"You can tell they have Russian military training from the way they built a bomb?" Verity said.

"Certainly you can," Bob Coulter said. "Russian, British, French, American — they're very different styles. Of course everyone thinks theirs is the best."

"Which *is* the best?" Joseph asked.

"British, of course!" Bob Coulter chuckled. "It depends what you're looking for. They've all got their strengths and weaknesses."

"No chance of any fingerprints, I suppose?" Tom asked.

"Alas no!" Salmon said. "Both clean as a whistle. They were very professional about that."

"Yes — they were professional about *that*," the chief superintendent said. "But I think we should also say that while we're clearly dealing with professional killers, they aren't the very *best* professional killers — or at least these explosives people aren't. The explosives were sophisticated and they evidently took care not to leave fingerprints, but taken overall the attempts on both our lives were sloppy."

"Not very well executed," Cecilia said before she could stop herself.

Verity giggled.

And... could she be deceiving herself, or was that a faint snicker of amusement over the speakerphone from Commander Salmon?

"And *that*," Davies continued, mercifully ignoring her, "was why Commander Salmon and I agreed that whoever was targeting us, if it was anything to do with the security services, it had to be someone who'd gone rogue."

"I don't follow," Joseph said.

"The thing is," the chief superintendent said, "if the actual security services were targeting us, they'd have sent people after us who'd have made sure we were dead."

"Oh. Right."

There was a slightly uncomfortable pause.

"Joseph," Cecilia said, "do you have anything?"

"I do. It's about those pages from the legal pad in Bernard Standish's study — the story he was working on."

She nodded. She had of course deposited the pad itself with the Met, since it was their case, but at her request they had at once sent photocopies of it to her own team.

"Well, Verity and I spent a lot of yesterday evening looking at them, and I think we've noticed a few things worth talking about."

"There's no 'we' about it," Verity said. "Joseph did the work. I merely contributed the occasional gesture of wifely encouragement."

"Rather more than that."

"Not really."

"Charming though this is," Cecilia said, "could you get on with it?"

Joseph grinned.

"Right. Well first, all those columns of figures — they're about money. Quite large sums being moved around. And it seems to involve something or someone called Dillon and Quincy, a financial services group, and another financial service group called Impresa Gabriella, which I gather is located in the Cayman Islands."

"Dillon and Quincy are indeed a financial services group," Ian Salmon said. "What may not be so obvious from their webpage or whatever is that they move a lot of money for the security services. Have done for years."

"Including back in 1986?" Joseph said.

"Certainly."

"Which," Davies said, "might explain why the security services would be interested in whatever story Bernard Standish was about to tell."

"It might," Salmon said.

"And what about Impresa Gabriella?" Cecilia asked.

"That," Salmon said, "is a financial service company in the Cayman Islands, as Mr Stirrup points out. What is, again, not so obvious from their publicity is that they're very closely tied to the Italian Mafia. To be precise, they're specialists in money laundering and tax evasion—which are, of course, major business enterprises in the Caymans anyway."

"Then there are names," Joseph said. "A lot of them! Some of them look to be Spanish or South American. Some sound to me Israeli. Others I think are Iranian. And most of them occur just two or three times. But there's one name that sounds quite British—Duncan Grimes. And that name is on every page."

"Duncan Grimes!" Salmon said. "We know about him. Organized crime. Mostly surplus weaponry and specialized import/export."

"Surplus weaponry?" Verity said. "Specialized import/export?"

"They're polite ways of saying he's an arms dealer and a smuggler," Bob Coulter said. "The two tend to go together."

"But he's not a contract killer?" Cecilia asked.

"I wouldn't say he's above having someone killed," Salmon said, "but no, I'd not say he's a hit man. He might employ one though."

She nodded.

"That's the trouble with criminals," he added. "They're so unethical."

She smiled.

There was a pause.

"That is indeed a very interesting collection of nationalities and artefacts you've discovered," Salmon continued. "If someone between 1985 and 1987 was dealing with the Israelis *and* the Iranians *and* South Americans *and* weapons *and* moving money, that says to me they were almost certainly involved in Iran-Contra."

"That occurred to us, too," Joseph said.

"Did it, indeed?" Salmon said. "Good for you."

"Iran-Contra?" Tom said. "That was an American thing, wasn't it?"

"The major scandal of the Reagan presidency," Salmon said. "I dare say Mr Stirrup and Detective Inspector Jones know the details."

Everyone looked at them. Verity looked at Joseph, who shrugged.

"The Reagan administration," he said, "enabled arms to be sold to Iran in exchange for hostages, and then used the profits to support the Contras—right wing militant groups in Nicaragua: which caused all hell to break loose when it came out, since Iran was under an arms embargo by the United States, and Congress had passed an amendment that prohibited funding the Contras. What made it even worse was that since 1983 American diplomats had been haranguing the rest of the world about how unethical it was to sell arms to Iran. So there was much egg on many faces."

"An admirable summary," Salmon said.

"And that," Joseph added, "if we're right, explains Standish's working title. 'US & I,' which doesn't mean, 'Us and I'. It's an abbreviation for, 'The United States and Iran'."

"All right, so what had all that to do with British Intelligence? Or the Mafia?" Headley asked.

Joseph exchanged a look with Verity, who shook her head. "Frankly," he said, "neither of us has the slightest idea."

"Mr Stirrup and Detective Inspector Jones," Salmon said, "are, I believe, merely pointing to the most obvious implication of the facts we have. But *if* someone from British intelligence and/or the

Mafia and/or this fellow Grimes were involved in the Iran-Contra business, and *if* that were the story Bernard Standish was going to tell, then one can imagine that quite a lot of people, British, American, and Italian, would have been rather pleased to see him silenced."

"The funny thing is," Joseph said, "you say you know about Duncan Grimes, and we did take a look at his record. But there's almost nothing there. I mean, a few convictions when he was young in the early 1980s, and since then some arrests on serious charges but he always manages to get off. Insufficient evidence, or the police procedure was wrong, or something else. But he always gets off."

"Which *could* mean," Verity said, "that he's got someone protecting him."

"Very possibly," Salmon said.

"In particular," Joseph continued, "there's nothing in Grimes' record to connect him with Iran-Contra. Nor in anything I've ever seen about Iran-Contra is there anything to suggest Grimes or any other British or Italian involvement. The middlemen seem to have been Israelis and expatriate Iranian businessmen."

"Well let's be clear," Verity countered. "There's nothing to suggest Grimes was involved, *except* these notes that Standish was working on and the fact that he died. Which again might suggest that Grimes and whoever's protecting him were clever enough to keep their heads down."

There was a pause.

"It certainly smells," Cecilia said, "but it's very full of 'ifs' and 'buts' and 'could means' and 'might suggests'. We need to do a lot of work. We need to get more facts."

"Ah!" Salmon said. "A wise police officer keeps our feet firmly on the ground."

Cecilia smiled. She was starting to get his style. That was his way of saying he agreed with her. Evidence was evidence, after all, and they had little or none. What you can't show, you don't know.

There was a pause.

"Well," the chief super said finally, as if reading her thought, "we do know that Grimes is named in Standish's notes, and we know he's a crook, even if a clever one. So as a start Sergeant Coulter and I can go and take a look at him. And your team can be following up on the Soames and Standish deaths from your end. You've got quite a few loose ends to look at."

She nodded.

"And I," Ian Salmon said, "can from my bed of pain and suffering see what is further to be learned about people who were involved in British Intelligence and with Messers Dillon and Quincy and Impresa Gabriella in 1986 or thereabouts. As our American friends say, it sounds like a plan."

FIFTEEN

Cecilia placed her hand over the speaker on her desk and looked at Verity.

"An interesting turn-up!" she said. "It's ex-Detective Superintendent Sterling, and he wants to talk to me." She returned to the phone. "Do you mind if I put you on speakerphone, Mr Sterling? My colleague Verity Jones is here too."

"I don't mind at all," he said. "She can hear us. That's fine."

"How can we help?" she said.

"Look, I've been talking with Sherri, and she thinks I ought to talk to you. About this Standish business, there's more to say—a lot more. The fact is, I've been holding out on you. I really thought I was doing the right thing, but since you told us about all those deaths, I don't see how I can be. I'm sorry. I know I've wasted a lot of your time and another journey to London must be a real pain for you. So Sherri and I were thinking we could come to Exeter on the train tomorrow, save you another trip, and then maybe I could talk to you then."

"Well as it happens, I'm planning to go up to London again

tomorrow with DI Jones. So why don't we just say we'll telephone you from Paddington Station when we arrive, and come over to you at your convenience?"

"Well if you're sure, that would be fine. I'd be really grateful. And I know I have some stuff you ought to know."

"I look forward to hearing it."

"I didn't know you were planning for us to go to London tomorrow," Verity said when the call was finished.

"I am now," Cecilia said. "Just a hunch. Anyway I like London. And trains."

The phone on her desk was flashing again.

She picked up.

It was Sergeant Stillwell, on the front desk.

"There's a Mrs Enid Soames here," he said, "to see whoever is in charge of investigating her husband's death. She arrived at Heathrow this morning, and she's driven straight here."

"Then please show her up at once," Cecilia said.

Enid Soames was a small, nicely dressed, attractive woman. She was probably, Cecilia thought, in her late forties or early fifties. She looked tired but calm and seemed entirely on top of things.

"I managed to book myself on the next flight home as soon as the police brought me the news," she said. "Then I rented a car at Heathrow and drove straight here."

Cecilia nodded.

"You and your husband were separated, Mrs Soames?"

Enid Soames shrugged.

"Not in any formal way. I suppose you could say we were one of those couples who aren't very good at living together and aren't very good at living apart. We'd still spend a few weeks together every year, and we'd talk most days in between on Skype or Face Time. I suppose I always had a vague hope we'd end up together again one day, somehow. Anyway, it won't happen now, will it?"

She paused.

"I suppose I'm here now because I'd like to help in any way I can—which I doubt is very much—with your investigation. And anyway I thought the least I could do for Charlie is be there for him to see to his funeral."

Cecilia nodded.

"Well, Mrs Soames," she said, "there are a few questions we were hoping to ask you. Of which the most obvious, I suppose, is can you think of any enemies your husband might have had, anyone who might have wanted him dead?"

Enid Soames shook her head. "Absolutely not. He was liked, so far as I could see, by most of the people who knew him. I was here last Christmas and he took me to a sort of end of term do that they had at the school—he taught maths at Alphington Grammar, but I'm sure you know that?"

Cecilia and Verity nodded again.

"Well, I was struck by what a nice, friendly bunch they all were—his colleagues and his students alike. They all seemed to get on well together. I dare say they had their strains—who doesn't? But there was certainly nothing apparent to me."

"What about his army days? Did he ever talk about that?"

"Sometimes. He'd been about and seen quite a lot—South Armagh, Germany, Belize. He did a stint in Bosnia just before he retired. And there were several pals he kept up with afterwards. But to be frank, Charlie's heart wasn't really in being a soldier. His family was military—there'd been three generations in the Devon and Dorsets. Naturally his dad hoped he'd follow the tradition. So I think there was a bit of pressure, maybe more than the family intended. Anyway, Charlie had a Short Service Commission and served seven years. But then he said, 'Look, Dad, I've done what you wanted me to do and I think I've made a decent shot at it. But now I'm retiring from the service rather than extending my Commission, and I'm going to do what I want to do and teach maths,' and that's what he did."

"Did you and Charlie meet while he was still in the army, Mrs Soames?" Verity asked.

"You mean, did I fall for the uniform?" She laughed and shook her head. "No, nothing like that. He was in his first year of teaching at the grammar school and I came in as a part-timer to do some art. That's how we met. What I fell for was a battered sports coat and cavalry twills."

She smiled as she spoke, but there was surely a tear in the corner of her eye.

Cecilia nodded. "We've talked of course with Charlie's colleagues at school. But do you think there are other people we should be getting in touch with? Other family? Those old army pals?"

She shook her head. "No other family, I'm afraid. We never had children. Just various neurotic dogs! Charlie's mum and dad died years ago, as did mine, and Charlie was an only child, like me. As for his army friends—I dare say one or two of them will want to come to his funeral if they can. But in any case I can let you have a note of who they are."

Again Cecilia nodded. "That would be very helpful," she said.

The two detectives looked at each other.

"Well, Mrs Soames," Cecilia said, "we very much appreciate your coming in to see us, and we grieve with you for your loss. I will certainly check with you if we do have further questions, but for the moment, so far as our investigation's concerned, I rather think you've given us all the help you can. Is there any way we can help you?"

"Yes there is," she said. "First, I'd like to see him."

"Of course," Cecilia said, "I can arrange that."

"And then, well, I know this sounds a bit pathetic, but the fact is I've never arranged a funeral before, and I'm not at all sure where to start. Does one go to see the vicar first, or the funeral agent? Charlie didn't go much, but he was always clear he was Church of England so he'd definitely want a Church of England service if that's possible. And is there a funeral agent in Exeter that you'd recommend rather than another? All these questions! I don't suppose you can you help with any of that, can you? Only I haven't a clue."

Cecilia smiled.

"Actually," she said, "I think I can. My husband's a priest." She looked at the clock. "I can call him now, if you like, I'm pretty sure he'll be at his desk. He knows all the ropes, and I'm sure he can get you started."

Enid Soames looked relieved. "That would be wonderful. And you'd don't think he'll mind that Charlie didn't go to church much?"

Again Cecilia smiled.

"I think," she said, "my husband will say that the church is your mother, which means she's always pleased to see you, whenever you turn up."

As Cecilia was leaving her office a little later, she passed Brenda Cosgrove—PC Brenda Cosgrove—standing gazing out of the window. Brenda Cosgrove had helped Michael and indeed the whole family on the night when Cecilia got shot, and was very good with animals, especially dogs. An attractive young woman, normally bright and bubbly, she looked today somewhat down, even disconsolate.

"Are you all right, Brenda?"

PC Cosgrove made a visible effort, and smiled.

"Oh, yes ma'am! I'm fine, thank you!"

"You're sure?"

"Oh, yes! Thank you, ma'am."

Cecilia nodded.

"Well, hang in there!"

"I'll do my best, ma'am."

Cecilia walked on. She'd seen Brenda out with Tom Wilkins on a couple of occasions last year. But not, come to think of it, lately. So perhaps they'd had a row?

She shook her head. It was surely none of her business anyway.

SIXTEEN

Exeter. St. David's Church of England School.
The same day, a little after 3.00 p.m.

H ere they came!
Michael, standing with the group of waiting parents, spotted Rachel at once among the tide of little people that erupted from the school. Already she showed signs of being tall for her age, long dark hair flying as she rushed up to him to be hugged.

"Did you have a good day in school?" he said. She'd only been going for a few weeks, but clearly loved it.

"Today we did arachnids," she announced as they walked back to the car, taking evident care to pronounce the last word just right.

"Did you, indeed!" he said. "Did you only do English spiders, or other kinds too?" There was no reason, he thought, why she should not know that he too knew what the word "arachnid" meant.

But she was way ahead of him.

"The word 'arachnid' does come from the Greek word for a spider," she informed him loftily, "and spiders *are* the biggest group of arachnids. But arachnids can be other things you know, like scorpions and ticks!"

"Can they now? Well, I never knew that!" And he really didn't, although to be fair it was hardly a question to which he'd given much thought.

"Susan Starr screamed when Mrs Leggett showed us a photo of a scorpion on the PowerPoint, but I told her not to be silly because a picture couldn't sting her."

"Did you? And what did she say to that?"

"She stopped screaming of course," Rachel said with the air of one who at the ripe age of six (going-on-thirty) took it for granted that when she spoke she would be taken notice of, since what she said was obviously right. "*And,*" she continued, bursting with newly-acquired knowledge, "most arachnids live on land but some live in the water."

"Goodness," he said. "And you learned all that at school today!"

"Absolutely!" she said.

He smiled. Imitation was, after all, the sincerest form of flattery and saying "absolutely" when she meant, "yes" was, as Cecilia pointed out to him the other day, definitely a habit Rachel had acquired from him.

They were back at the car now, where Figaro greeted them with waving tail.

"Daddy," Rachel said suddenly, after he'd buckled her in and just as he was preparing to start the car.

"Yes, sweetheart?"

"Why is Figaro getting grey hairs round his mouth?"

"Because he's getting old, sweetheart."

As soon as Michael said that, it occurred to him where this conversation might go. He hoped it didn't.

But he could see Rachel considering. He could almost watch the wheels turning. That was the trouble with having a child who was too smart for her own comfort.

"Daddy..." she said slowly.

"Yes, sweetheart?"

"That means Figaro's going to die some day, doesn't it?"

"Well, not for a very long time yet, we hope. That's why we try to take the best care of him we can."

Rachel was not, however, to be put off.

"But Figaro *is* going to die? Some day?"

He *so* didn't want to deal with this just now. He wanted to go home for tea. But then if he didn't deal with it, why should she ever bother to ask him about anything that mattered to her again?

He sighed, gave up thinking about starting the car and going home for tea, sat back in the driver's seat, and looked at her.

"Sweetheart," he said, "Everybody has to die some day."

"Including granddad and grandma and you and mummy and Rosie?"

"Yes. But not for long time yet, we hope."

He was repeating himself.

"But mummy almost died when that man shot her, didn't she?"

The child was merciless. She would have the truth.

"Yes, sweetheart, mummy nearly died."

There was a long pause.

Should he say something else? Was it time to talk about how we must be nice to each other while we still have each other? What would a six-year-old understand? What do any of us understand?

"And then," she said, "when we die we'll be with God?"

"Yes, sweetheart."

"Which will be nice for us?"

"I believe it will be more nice than we can possibly imagine."

"Will Figaro be with God too?"

"Of course Figaro will be with God."

God doesn't make anything disposable.

"But we mustn't try to go 'til God calls us, because there are things to do here?"

"That's right."

She nodded.

"Good. I thought it was like that. Stanley Bradshaw at school said dogs don't have souls and can't go to heaven. But I told him he was wrong."

I'll bet you did.

"Are we going home for tea, now?"

"Yes, sweetheart. Grandma's making some of those jam things you like."

"Good. Figaro likes them, too."

He started the car, glancing at her out of the corner of his eye as he did so.

She was looking out of the car window, the afternoon sun shining on her hair. Dear God, she was so beautiful. It almost broke his heart.

And in the event he'd got off pretty lightly.

As for the little matter of death...

It seemed to him that at present his daughter was at least as well prepared for that as he was.

SEVENTEEN

Exeter, St. Mary's Rectory.
That evening.

"So I sent you a customer today!" Cecilia said to Michael as, children and animals duly dealt with, they were putting away the supper things.

"You did. Thank you. She's a nice woman."

"I assume there's no problem helping her with the funeral?"

"None at all. Your folk have said they're ready to release the body, and I made arrangements for her with Jim Cameron" — Cameron & Cameron was the funeral agent with whom Michael normally dealt — "to have the funeral on Tuesday morning."

"Do you know where it will be?"

Cecilia's general practice was to attend the funerals of victims in cases she was dealing with.

"At Saint Bede's" — the little village church of Haldon — "Enid Soames was very clear her husband would want to be buried from a church, not a chapel in a funeral home. 'He was very traditional like that,' she said. So I phoned the team rector and she was happy for it to happen in the church. And as I'm free that morning and I've got to know Enid a bit I'm going to take it. I gather he was well liked in the village and the school where he taught, so I think there'll be quite a big turn out. We picked the readings and she knows a couple of people who were Charlie's friends who'll do them and the intercessions. She used to come over from Canada and stay for a few weeks every year, so she actually knows quite a lot of people here."

"She told me that."

"The organ at St. Bede's is reasonable, and George says he'll play," —George was Michael's regular organist and choir master at St. Mary's—"so we'll have some hymns."

"Charlie's favourites?" Cecilia asked.

This was something of a running joke with them. When arranging funerals Michael was frequently frustrated by families' insisting on the deceased's "favourite hymns," said hymns often being (at least in his view) completely unsuitable for the occasion. That said, since he regarded a funeral service as at least in part for the comfort and sustenance of the mourners, to help them grieve as they needed, he never had the heart to take a completely hard line, and so after making his suggestions usually swallowed his frustration and went along more or less with what they wanted— which on this occasion hadn't been too hard.

"She asked for 'O thou who camest from above' to *Hereford*," he said, "which although it's not what I would have picked is certainly not *un*suitable."

"I love that one."

One of the things Cecilia had discovered since being married to a priest was that she actually enjoyed singing hymns... well, some hymns.

"Me too, so that's all right."

"And surely the last verse is bang on for a funeral? 'Til death thy endless mercies seal' and all that?"

"You're right. And we're going to have 'Jesu, Son of Mary' to Schulz's tune, and the Contakion."

"Will the people be up to that?"

"When I showed them to her she liked the words—which shows she has good taste. And George is going to bring along a couple of pals who are singers. They can be at the back and keep it going. And both hymns will be in the bulletin with the music for those who can read it."

"What about after the service?"

"I booked the village hall with the rector and then I phoned Elsie Morgan and she's going to cater a little fruitcake and sherry reception." Elsie was the person he usually recommended for such events—reasonably priced, but always of good quality. "She's willing to be flexible about numbers, which is good. So Mrs Soames will just have to pay for those who come!"

"It's all obviously completely organized. Haven't you been a busy chap!"

He laughed.

"It was easy enough. Like most people who have to organize funerals for people they care about, I think Enid Soames just wanted someone who knew the ropes to be in charge so she didn't have to be."

"I think," she said, "that some people also like to have their funerals organized by people who aren't intimidated by the dread visitor."

"The dread visitor?"

"Death."

He stared at her.

"You're right," he said after a moment. "We aren't intimidated by death." He paused, as if remembering something. "Or at least, we've no business to be, given what we profess." Again he hesitated. "I suppose that's one of the reasons I like to persuade people, if I can, to have the great funeral hymns rather than just their favourites. Those hymns make it very clear that the church takes death seriously but refuses to be intimidated by it."

There was a pause while he poured them both more coffee.

"So what have you been up to?" he said.

"Still battling with poor Soames' murder, I'm afraid. It's getting more and more complicated."

She told him of the latest developments — as was her usual practice. She knew she could rely on his discretion and in more than one case in the past she'd made a breakthrough as a direct result of his coming back at her. On this occasion, however, he had nothing to offer beyond the equivalent of Alice's "curiouser and curiouser."

On another matter, to her surprise, he had rather more to say.

"Incidentally, you remember Brenda Cosgrove?" she said. "The nice PC who helped with Figaro and everything the night I got shot?"

"I'm not likely to forget."

"Well, she seemed very down in the dumps today. She puts a good face on it — she's not a whiner — but something's bothering her."

Michael smiled and shook his head.

"No great mystery there," he said.

"Really?"

"I imagine she's anxious about Bob Coulter."

"Bob Coulter? Why should she be anxious about him?"

"I expect she's missing him. And worried about him."

"What? Are you saying they're an item?"

"That's right."

"I thought she was going out with Tom Wilkins?"

He laughed. "You're way out of date! Tom and Brenda went out together a few times last year, but they were just friends. Brenda and Bob Coulter have really got together since then. Quite hot and heavy, if I'm not mistaken! And I don't think I am."

"Isn't he a bit old for her?" she said.

"He's 36. She's 23. One year less gap than your mama and papa, and they seem to have made it work."

She smiled. "I suppose they have."

"Bob Coulter's a bit grizzled, I grant you, but I guess he's just one of those people who gets grey early."

"And there was me thinking he was a committed bachelor."

"So was Benedict."

"Touché."

She shook her head and sighed. "Still I wonder—how on earth is it that you know all this and I don't? I mean—you are at the station, I suppose, at most a couple of hours each week, mostly to collect me, and I'm there all the time."

He chuckled.

"A vital part of being a parish priest is knowing who's going out with whom."

"But this isn't exactly your parish, is it? I'm still amazed that you noticed in the short time you're there."

He considered for a moment.

"Your job," he said finally, "is to pay attention to people who are doing weird things like killing each other. Mine's to pay attention to people who are doing rather ordinary things like falling in love. Actually, I think I got the better deal."

EIGHTEEN

West London, Praed Street.
The following morning,
Saturday, 24th September

"There!" Glyn Davies said, peering at the photographs he had on his phone and then up again, "that's them. The short one is Duncan Grimes and the tall one is his chief of staff, Mitch McClintock."

As they watched, an elegant black Bentley limousine (but then, he asked himself, when are Bentleys not elegant?) had just deposited Grimes and McClintock at the entrance to Hilton Paddington Station Hotel, once the Royal Great Western and still, in appearance at least, retaining some of its Victorian glory.

"I gather," Davies said, "there's a daily routine. Grimes holds court in his suite, and McClintock sits in what's called the Steam Bar and vets anyone who wants to see him."

He and Bob Coulter were parked in a rental car across the road from the hotel with a good view of it. Praed Street was as busy as it ever is with morning traffic, but warrant cards have their uses, and to be left alone they had needed only once to flash them at the traffic warden.

"It would be good to watch him at it," Coulter said after a minute. "Why don't I go in while you stay here?"

"You think you look respectable enough?"

Coulter chuckled. "They'll know I'm a gentleman as soon as I speak to them. Anyway, it's a Hilton. Money talks and we're on expenses, aren't we?"

Davies laughed. "Go to it, then."

Coulter had nursed his cocktail and a bowl of nuts for some twenty minutes and watched McClintock as he sat at the bar with a drink he never touched looking at a magazine whose page he never turned. During this vigil two people had come into the bar, walked up to him, and were waved on with no more than a glance. Presumably regulars. Then McClintock took a call on his mobile. He listened for several moments, nodded, put the phone back into a side pocket of his jacket, and looked expectantly toward the entrance. Almost at once a tall, well-dressed man in a dark suit entered and came across to him. The two bent towards each other, and began talking earnestly.

It would be nice to know what they were saying.

But then, one of the glories of modern technology is that everyone who has a mobile phone also has a highly effective bug if they choose to use it like that.

Bob Coulter picked up his own mobile, and made a call.

"See what you can hear," he said softly.

He glanced around him, saw that he was not observed, then bent and with a gentle flick slid the phone over the carpet so that it came to rest just under McClintock's barstool. He sat back and ate another peanut.

The two men continued their quiet conversation for several minutes—mostly, it seemed, McClintock listening while the other conveyed information to him. Finally, McClintock wrote something down, and nodded. They both stood and shook hands. And the visitor left. McClintock made a call on his mobile, no more than a couple of words, put the phone back into the side pocket of his jacket, picked up the magazine, and resumed his vigil by the bar.

After a moment or two a waiter came by with a tray of drinks. As he did so, Bob Coulter rose casually to his feet, bent to retrieve something from his table, and as he did so caught the passing tray with his elbow, so that tray and drinks shot onto the carpet in the direction of McClintock's stool.

"I'm *terribly* sorry!" he said. "That was entirely my fault."

Which was undoubtedly the truth.

"Of course I'll pay for the drinks," he said. "Here, let me help."

He leaned towards the scattered glasses.

"Not at all, sir," the waiter said courteously. "Don't trouble yourself. Accidents will happen."

"Well, if you're sure."

"Absolutely no problem, sir."

His phone safely recovered, and having apologized to McClintock, against whom he had brushed as he got to his feet, Bob Coulter sauntered out.

"What did you get?" he said when he was back in the car. "Could you hear anything?"

"Actually I could, though I'm not sure what it all meant. One man was clearly telling another about a scheduled delivery of something. He never said what—obviously they both knew. But he mentioned Bristol, and something he called *La Luna Rossa*. '*La Luna Rossa* as before,' he said. Would that be a restaurant? A club?"

"Maybe it's a ship? After all, Bristol's a port."

"That's true. Then he gave him a series of letters and numbers to write down. Luckily for us he was rather anxious that the other one had it right, so he spelled it out and repeated it—and here it is." He showed Coulter: a series of four letters, followed by six digits, followed by combination of three letters and a digit. "Any idea what that means?"

Coulter shook his head. "Not a clue."

"And then I gathered one of them left, and then the one who didn't leave made a very short phone call. All he said was, 'It's on.' It'd be nice to know who he was calling."

"Then I can maybe help with that," Coulter said. "Here's his phone."

Davies eyebrows shot up.

"It was in his jacket pocket, hanging loose. He was practically begging me to take it. And your Commander Salmon said while we're working for the security services normal rules for gathering evidence don't apply. We're here to get intelligence by any reasonable means. Well, I thought that was pretty reasonable. He never even noticed."

"All right, all right. I get it." Davies shook his head. He must try to stop thinking like a police officer. This really *was* starting to feel like the old days.

"Time to call Joseph," he said.

Joseph was evidently at his desk and answered immediately.

"First," Davies said, "we need to know about something called *La Luna Rossa*, in Bristol. What would it be? A restaurant? A club?" He looked at Coulter. "A ship, maybe?"

"I'm checking. Hang on sir. There's an Italian beer—brewed by Birrificio del Ducato ... I'm cross-referencing with Bristol... nobody seems to stock it there... Ah, yes, there's a pizza place... no, sorry, that's in Orsay... wait a minute... Bristol, you say? I think it *is* a ship. Here you are. It's in dock now... in the Royal Portbury... *La Luna Rossa*, a container vessel... Italian owned, Panamanian registry. Is that what you want?"

Davies and Coulter looked at each other.

"I think," Davies said, "it could very well be what we want. The next thing is, we have a long combination of groups of letters and numbers. This is it."

He read it out.

"Do you have any idea what that might be about?"

Joseph chuckled.

"That's easy sir—especially since we've just decided *La Luna Rossa* is a container ship. That's an identification code for a container. It'll be on the outside, on the doors at the end—generally top right hand side as you look at it, if I'm not mistaken."

He paused. "Do you want more?"

"Anything you've got."

"Okay. The first four letters indicate the owner and the product. The six digits that follow are the registration number. The extra digit is what they call the check digit. And the last group—the sequence of four letters and digits—indicates the size and type of container. In your case—45G1—'4' and '5' mean it's forty feet long and five feet high, and 'G1' says it's a general purpose container."

"Right," Davies said. "So from the initial four letters, you can tell us who owns this particular container, can you?"

"I should be able to. Though of course the owner of the container probably won't be the owner of the contents."

"I understand that."

"It's coming up... Avon Shipping Services. That's a Bristol company."

"That makes sense, I suppose."

"And... just a minute sir." A pause. "They've got some protection, but nothing I can't deal with." They could hear Joseph's fingers on his keyboard. "Yes... all right... I'm in! I'm looking at Avon's files now... cross-referencing the check number... here we are... that particular container is contracted to something called 'Shell Associates'... which is clearly nothing to do with several other companies by that name... hahaha, a shell called shell, bit blatant that, don't you think? And they are... wait a minute, there are half a dozen more shells... but their protection is pathetic... there it is! The *real* owners of the contents are Messers Dillon and Quincy. According to Avon's records the contents are 'financial documentation,' whatever that is. Dillon and Quincy are the financial services people, aren't they?"

"That's exactly what they are."

"*La Luna Rossa* took the container on board for them at Umm Qasr in Iraq on the 28th July—about six weeks ago."

"Iraq?"

"That's right."

Bob Coulter nodded. "It makes sense. It's the only large container port in the country. Ten to one it's weapons."

"It could be stolen artefacts from the museums. There's a huge market in that at the moment."

"Well whatever it is," Joseph continued, "the container's now been unloaded in Bristol and is on Alberta Quay, Berth 2, in the General Products Terminal. Luckily it's on the ground, not stacked, so access is no problem. That's all I can tell at the moment. I'll keep tracking it, in case they move it or something else comes up."

"Good. Excellent. Now, here's a different thing altogether. We got hold of a smartphone belonging to one of the villains. With that we can find out who he just called, can't we?"

Joseph laughed out loud.

"Your villain must be vain about his tech. If he was wise, he'd have a disposable phone and change it every week."

"So you can do something with this?"

"Smartphones are a hacker's dream, sir."

"What about his password?"

"You don't need it if you know what you're doing. Do you have the extra mobile I gave you? And the connectors?"

"I do."

"And what kind of smartphone is the villain's?"

Davies told him.

"Then you need the yellow connector. Use it to connect my mobile to it."

"Done."

"Now—when you did that the screen on my mobile lit up, yes?"

"It did."

"Top row, middle button, says 'Download and forward'."

"Got it."

"Touch that, sir."

He did.

Instantly the screen changed: "Downloading... Forwarding..." for several seconds; then "Upload complete."

"Good," Joseph said. "I've got it all. The last call he made was at 10.29 a.m. today. It was fourteen seconds long, and it was to...." He read out the digits, evidently typing them into his computer as he did so. Then he said, "Here we are! It was to a suite rented to Mr Duncan Grimes at the Hilton Paddington Station Hotel in London W2."

No surprise there, then.

"It'll take me a while to go through all this," Joseph continued. "But he's had the phone since June and with what you've just sent me I can see every number he's ever called on it and everyone who's ever called him. I can't tell the content of the calls but I can tell their duration. I'll let you know what I find."

"That's terrific Joseph—"

"Sir, there is just one other thing. Can you by any chance get the phone back to him without him knowing it's been nicked?"

He looked at Bob Coulter. "Maybe."

"Well sir, just let me do something. You've still got it connected to mine, haven't you?"

"Yes Joseph."

"Right. Just hang on, will you?"

Davies watched as the screen on Joseph's mobile went black; then read, "Uploading..."; and then, "Upload complete."

"Right sir, now disconnect."

He did so.

"Okay. So long as that phone remains on planet earth, I can now track it, and I can listen to and record any conversation on it. So if you *could* get it back to him without him realizing..."

Davies nodded.

"We'll work on it, Joseph. In any case, brilliant!"

"Nothing to it, sir. As I keep telling Verity, this is the age of the computer nerd!"

Nineteen

As Cecilia and Verity emerged from Queens Park Tube Station at a few minutes after eleven, a police car passed them at high speed followed by an ambulance, lights flashing and sirens blaring, northward along the Salusbury Road, and then left with squealing tyres at the next corner.

They looked at each other.

Verity frowned.

"As they're always saying in *Star Wars*," she said, "I've got a bad feeling about this."

Cecilia nodded.

They followed, turning left at the corner.

Something was happening in Kingswood Avenue.

Thirty or so yards, and now they turned right. And there was the pleasant Victorian house and garden they'd visited on Thursday, surrounded by emergency vehicles — police, fire, ambulance.

And in their midst smoke and the stink of explosive.

Cecilia and Verity approached slowly, starting to produce

their warrant cards—which were not needed, for the officer in charge recognized them from their visit to Paddington Green Station earlier in the week.

"Detective Superintendent Cavaliere," he said, "Detective Inspector Jones. I'm afraid we have a situation on our hands."

"What's happened?" Cecilia said.

"It was fifteen or so minutes ago. Greg Sterling's car was booby-trapped. His daughter says he'd just gone out to it to get some papers he'd left in it. The bomb must have been pressure activated. It went off when he sat in the driver's seat. He'll have died instantly. That's the only good thing about it. That and the fact that no one else was hurt, which is a miracle."

"Oh, dear God," Cecilia said, "how awful."

This surely wouldn't have happened if we hadn't come round asking questions.

"We had an appointment with him," she said, "but I think we'd better leave. I dare say I'm the last person on earth the family wants to see just now."

"Wrong," he said. "They *do* want to see you. His daughter Sherri told me you were coming. Come through."

"All right," she said.

He led them through the crowd, past the ugly, twisted wreckage that reeked of death, and up to the house.

Sherri must have seen them, for she was at the door, pale and serious, but calm.

"Come in," she said.

"I'm afraid this must be my fault—"

"Of course it's not your fault. It's the fault of the bastards that did it. You're just trying to do your job. Come in. I need to talk to you."

Sherri led them into the pleasant living room with the model of the *Cutty Sark*, where a man in a tweed sports coat was sitting. He at once got to his feet.

"This is Joe, my husband. I'm going to make us all a nice cup of tea. Then we can talk."

Cecilia nodded her acquiescence, as did Verity.

This, she thought, is what the English do when they are under attack. They make themselves nice cups of tea. Well, it got them through the Blitz, didn't it?

"She had the kettle on already," Joe explained. "She'll only be a minute. Would you like to sit down?"

They murmured thanks and sat. Cecilia could think of nothing to say that didn't seem fatuous or self-serving, so she didn't say it. Verity did the same. They remained thus for several minutes.

Sherri bustled back with the tea, milky and sweet. The odd thing was, it worked.

"Now," she said, "I've a lot to tell you. Can you record this, Detective Superintendent Cavaliere? On tape or something?"

"I can if you want," Cecilia said.

"I do. Daddy told us everything last night—everything he was planning to tell you, and I want to do the best I can to make sure it doesn't get lost in case someone decides to be on the safe side and bump me and Joe off, too."

Cecilia nodded, switched her mobile to record, and placed it on the table.

"Why don't you do the same?" she said to Verity. "Then we'll have a backup."

The two mobiles in place, Sherri began her father's story.

"When the Standish thing came in," she said, "there was no lack of witnesses."

"It doesn't look like that from the file," Verity said.

"I dare say it doesn't. I'll get to that in a minute. Look, let me tell it in my own way, will you? And then you can ask me questions when I've finished. Okay?"

Verity nodded. "Okay. Sorry."

"Two things about this case struck dad as strange from the

start. First, as he told you, although Standish's lad was quite sure someone had pulled him back from the road and saved his life, no one would say it was them. Second, the witnesses couldn't seem to put together a decent description of the car. It was big and it was dark, maybe black. That was about all they agreed on. One witness called it massive. Another said clumsy. Some thought it was American. Others thought it wasn't. Several said it was a limo. But *no one* could put a make to it. It was as if it was a kind of car no one had ever seen before."

The others nodded.

"Now here's what you don't know. Dad was a bit of a car buff himself, and it struck him that one car that might actually fit this description, such as it was, would be a Russian Zil limousine— huge and clumsy, and a bit like an American car but sort of different. And of course no one would recognize the make, because the chances were none of the witnesses would ever have seen one before, since dad was pretty sure there was only one such car in England at the time, and it belonged to the Russian Embassy. Which would of course mean that if the car *was* theirs, there'd be nothing the police could do about the hit and run because the driver would claim diplomatic immunity. Still, dad thought it would be at least nice to know. So he actually sent for photos of a Zil limo that he could show the witnesses, to see if they rang any bells."

Everyone nodded.

"Right. That was dad's progress down one track. But there was another track altogether. Dad knew that Standish was an investigative journalist—well, everyone did—and of course he'd heard of people wanting to shut investigative journalists up if they were about to print something inconvenient. Still, overall he wasn't much of a one for conspiracy theories—'Remember Occam's razor!' he'd say 'The simplest explanation's generally the right one!'"

Verity nodded approvingly.

"So though the idea of Standish being murdered occurred to him, he didn't think it very likely. That was until he went round to Standish's home and checked his study, and found on his desk what looked like a more or less finished article about rogue elements in MI6 being involved in an illegal arms deal between the Americans and the Iranians, and creaming off massive profits. When he read that, and considered the fuss it might cause, he began to ask himself whether someone really *might* have wanted Standish silenced, and been willing to kill him to see it happened. He at once took the article into evidence."

Cecilia and Verity looked at each other. So Greg Sterling had by no means made a mistake over the significance of Standish's notes. He'd taken into evidence the text that showed conclusively what Standish was working on. And of course he'd had no need of the preparatory notes because he had the article itself.

Perhaps because she was a policeman's daughter, Sherri was a good witness. Occasionally she stopped to check a point with her husband, but for the most part she told her father's story without help.

His suspicions aroused, he'd conferred with senior officers. Two hours later, one of those officers told him that someone from the security services would be arriving to consult with him that afternoon. At the appointed time, someone turned up: a man in his middle forties, well dressed, well educated.

The man confirmed that he was indeed from the security services, which Sterling believed, since he could only have had clearance to talk to a police officer about an on-going investigation from someone very senior in the Met, and presumably such clearance was not given lightly. The man then told him point blank that on no account was the Standish investigation to be pursued and that interests involving the very highest level of national security were involved. Standish's unfinished article, together with the witness statements, were to be handed over immediately, and the inquiry to be closed "for lack of evidence." DI Sterling's failure to pursue the inquiry would, he was assured, in no way reflect on him nor would it affect his career. He was simply doing his patriotic duty.

Sterling was so taken aback by these requests that he actually insisted on consulting with his own superiors, who assured him, however, that his orders to concur with everything the man from the security services asked came from the very highest level in the chain of command.

So he concurred. He handed over the witness statements and the article, even though it meant stripping the file on Standish's death to a barely adequate minimum—as Cecilia and Verity had noticed when they looked at it.

Following this, everything happened as the security services man said it would. There was no reprimand or fallout for his failure to pursue the inquiry, and in time he became involved in other cases and forgot about it.

Until his young ex-colleagues told him of the new development last week. That had disturbed him. And then Cavaliere and Jones came to him on Thursday with a story of mayhem that left him seriously doubting what he had been told thirty years earlier. Finally, after consulting with his daughter he'd decided that come what may, he must level with officers who were investigating the matter now, and had phoned them. The rest they knew.

"You know," Sherri said to Cecilia as they were taking their leave at the front door, "you almost certainly saved my life by deciding to come to London today."

"How did I do that?"

"Because if Dad and I'd been going to Exeter together, I'd have gone out to the car with him and we'd have got in it together. I just think you ought to know that."

Cecilia nodded. "Thank you."

What else could she say?

As they were leaving the street, officers were starting to clear the debris from the road, carefully loading the blackened and twisted remnants of Sterling's car onto a trailer.

Cecilia paused for a moment to watch.

A man had died in that debris... a decent man who'd tried to do his duty... whose daughter teased him because he still noticed a pretty woman... who made model ships with his grandchildren.

And but for the grace of God his daughter would have died there too, leaving her children motherless and her husband a widower.

Her mouth tightened.

> *I was not angry since I came to France*
> *Until this instant.*

She looked at Verity.

"We've got to get these creeps, Verity."

"We'll do our best, ma'am."

She nodded.

In some ways, Headley was right. This job was easier when you hated the bad guys.

Which didn't mean you did it better or that it was right.

As her beloved Jane Austen pointed out, "angry people are not always wise."

Cecilia sighed, and walked on.

"By the way," she said after a few more minutes, by way of changing the subject to something more cheerful, "did you know that Bob Coulter is going out with Brenda Cosgrove?"

"Everyone knows that," Verity said.

TWENTY

London. The Hilton Paddington Station Hotel.
The same morning, a few minutes later.

McClintock was still on his stool by the bar when Glyn Davies wandered into the Steam Bar and took his seat at a nearby table, just out of his quarry's line of sight. The place was still quiet. After a moment he looked round to see that he wasn't observed, then bent down and flicked something across the carpet towards the barstools.

He sat back and ate a peanut. After a few minutes, a waiter bustled in, saw him, and came over.

"What can I bring you, sir?"

He ordered a drink.

"And by the way," he said, indicating the bar, "that looks like someone's mobile phone on the floor by the bar."

"It does indeed sir. I'll go and check. That gentleman's been there for some time, so it may be his. Perhaps it fell out of his pocket."

"Perhaps it did."

"That Joseph is an amazing lad," Coulter said when the chief superintendent got back to the car fifteen or so minutes later. "We were watching *The Lion in Winter* the other night and then wondered if any of it was true. It took me the best part of a quarter of an hour just to find out from Google who Eleanor of Aquitaine was. So how does Joseph manage to do all that stuff *in seconds?*"

Davies chuckled. "I rather suspect I *so* don't want to know the answer to that question! But here's a question I do want answered. We've both had our guesses, but I really would like to know for sure what kind of 'financial documentation' a financial services company is moving from Iraq that needs a container forty feet long and five feet high to hold it."

Bob Coulter grinned.

"There's one sure way to find out," he said. He looked at his watch. "We could be in Bristol in just over two hours. I wonder what kinds of surveillance systems the port has?"

"Human surveillance I dare say we can dodge. As for electronic—let's talk to Joseph again."

"Give me a couple of hours to work on it," Joseph said when they called him. "By the time you're in Bristol I should know what you're up against and have some suggestions."

"Excellent," Glyn Davies said when the call was over. "So let's have some lunch and then go for it. After a morning of eating peanuts and pretending to drink, I'm absolutely starving!"

Driving to Bristol to inspect the dock and the container seemed like a good plan when they made it.

Three or so hours later, however, some miles past Swindon, Glyn Davies sat back in the driver's seat, exchanged a look with

Bob Coulter and sighed. Robert Burns was, alas, right: "The best laid schemes o' mice an' men / Gang aft a-gley" — and this was one of them. One of those sudden mists that roll in on occasion from the Bristol Channel and the Severn Estuary had blanketed the motorway in fog and brought the heavy afternoon traffic first to a crawl, and finally to a standstill. Evening was now coming on. In addition to the fog, they were informed that an articulated lorry had overturned a mile or so in front of them. The road was likely to be blocked for some time.

"This is hopeless," he said. "There's an exit just ahead. I suggest we call Joseph and tell him we're stuck. Then let's get off here, and try to find a pub or something where we can get a drink and something to eat and somewhere to stay for the night."

"I'm for that," Bob Coulter said.

TWENTY-ONE

Heavitree Police Station,
Sunday, 25th September

As soon as Cecilia and Verity arrived back from London, late on Saturday afternoon, Cecilia copied all members of the Serious Crimes Team with the recording of Sherri Mason's narrative. At the same time she indicated that she wanted a team meeting in her office at eight-thirty the following morning.

So on Sunday she kissed Michael goodbye at about half past seven as he was heading for the church, said, "Say one for me this morning, please!" and herself headed for the Heavitree Police Station, which she entered at about eight o'clock pretty much as if it had been a regular weekday.

Joseph and Verity were just ahead of her. Joseph looked to be in pain and was limping badly, leaning heavily on his stick.

"I'll just get my notes and check downstairs," he said. "See you in a minute."

Cecilia looked quizzically at Verity after he had gone.

"Bad night?" she said.

"Yes. But don't ask him about it!"

"Got it!"

When they first knew him, Joseph had been permanently confined to a wheel chair, the result of the car crash that killed his parents when he was thirteen. But then in 2012 new surgical techniques followed by extensive physiotherapy had brought him to a point where he was able to get about quite well with a stick. That was the good news. The bad news was that from time to time—especially if he became overtired—his back and his hip would still cause him serious pain.

But he also hated sympathy from anyone except Verity, and Cecilia had long since learned not to offend him with it.

"And just at the moment he won't take his painkillers," Verity added. "He says, 'They work all right, but I think they make me less sharp, and I hate it. This is a big case. I need to be on top.' The best way to cheer him up will be to get him to tell us about what he was working on last night!"

"Well I certainly intend to do that," Cecilia said.

The team gathered in her office.

"Let's look at what's come in over the last twenty-four hours," she said. "Joseph, I believe you've got something for us?"

"I think I have," he said.

It seemed to Cecilia no cause for wonder that he had arrived at the station exhausted for as was soon apparent he had spent the greater part of the previous evening going item by item through the information he'd downloaded from McClintock's phone.

Most of the phone numbers were obvious enough, including many calls from and to Duncan Grimes, and they learned nothing there. There was, however, one number that Joseph could not trace. The call had lasted only four seconds, and he reckoned it was most likely from a disposable mobile phone. In which case it would be virtually impossible to trace.

"The one thing I could do is call it back," he said. "Maybe pretend I've dialled it by accident and got a wrong number. That might flush them out."

"But then if whoever-it-is really is anything to do with this, calling them might be precisely what makes them nervous so they decide to change phones," Cecilia said. "Let's see if the chief super or Salmon have any thoughts, but my instinct for the moment is to wait until we really have some idea whose number it might be. Then it might be a weapon—depending on how long they keep it."

"Of course it could *actually* have been a wrong number," Verity pointed out.

"It could," Cecilia said. What we can't show, we don't know.

McClintock had also received a couple of calls last evening from Duncan Grimes, and thanks to Joseph's tracking device, the team were able to listen to these.

"Lucio Di Stefano's been asked to work with us again," Grimes said.

"O Christ, do we have to have the Italians in on it again?"

"Looks like it. Di Stefano's flying in on Thursday or Friday to take a look. We're not sure which night yet, so you'll need to have the lads ready for either."

"Bugger it. They're not going to like hanging around."

"It's what we pay them for."

"Who's Lucio Di Stefano?" Tom and Headley asked almost together after they'd listened to this exchange.

"He's Mafia," Joseph said. "A *capo dei capi*. And if what I found out about him last night is right, even among *capi dei capi* he's a big deal. He lives in a kind of semi-fortress in Sicily. He's old now and doesn't travel much, so if he's willing to come and oversee this business in person, it must be very serious. His speciality is money laundering. Do you remember Impresa Gabriella, the holding company in the Caymans that cropped up in Bernard Standish's 1986 notes? The one we said had ties to the Mafia? Well, that's Di Stefano's. He named it after his late wife."

"So," Cecilia said slowly, "we now have two events, the Iran-Contra thing in 1986 and this container thing, thirty years apart but involving at least two of the same players—Duncan Grimes and Impresa Gabriella slash Lucio Di Stefano."

"It could be *three* of the same players," Verity said. "Grimes said Di Stefano had 'been asked' to work with them. That sounds to me as though someone else did the asking. Grimes is just doing what he's told. There's a boss."

"Of course!" Headley said. "A Mr Big!"

"Or a Ms," Verity said. "But yes."

"It could be the unknown number that called McClintock was the boss," Tom said. "It could be they normally call Grimes but for some reason that day they couldn't get him. So they left a quick message with Grimes's sidekick instead."

"It *could* be," Verity said.

Tom grinned. "Or of course it could be a wrong number!"

"All right," Headley said, "so it's looks from what Grimes said on the phone as though he's working for someone *now*, but does that necessarily mean he was working for the same person thirty years ago?"

There was a pause, which Verity broke.

"No," she said, "it doesn't. I hate to admit it, but whatever Grimes and company and their unknown boss are up to now in Bristol could be absolutely nothing to do with whatever they were up to thirty years ago. Which would mean that it also had nothing to do with the murders we're investigating, which clearly *are* linked to what happened thirty years ago."

"All right," Cecilia said after a moment, "so we *could* actually be investigating two different crimes, unrelated apart from the fact that some of the same people are involved in them. So now let's bring into all this what we got yesterday—Sherri Mason's account of her dad's 1986 investigation and what happened to it. You've all listened to the recording of what she said, I trust?"

Everyone nodded.

"So, what did you think? On the whole, do we trust that account?"

"It sounds pretty plausible to me," Headley said. "She sounded like a good witness."

There were general nods of agreement.

"I trust it too," Cecilia said. "All right then. Here's what Sherri's story, taken together with everything else we know, says to me so far—and please stop me if at any point you think I'm going beyond the evidence. First, whatever was going on in 1986 that led to the death of Bernard Standish had behind it someone influential enough to pull some massive strings. Just look at what they could do! They were able in the first place to orchestrate a slice for themselves of a colossal fraud involving foreign money, illegal arms sales and all the shenanigans that was the Iran-Contra affair. They were then able to authorize a black bag op utilizing Sandhurst cadets to see whether anyone was onto them. They were *then* able to arrange for the journalist Bernard Standish's death when it appeared that he *was* onto them—very probably using the services of a foreign embassy."

"Very possibly using the services of the *Russian* embassy," Tom pointed out. "Which is interesting since we've already noticed a Russian connection in some of our current killings."

"Your point is taken," Cecilia said. "And finally they had enough clout to stop an ongoing police investigation in its tracks when it seemed to be getting close to them—in the name of national security. Now—have I gone beyond what's implicit in Sherri's story and what we already knew?"

There was silence, and a shaking of heads.

"Which being so, I ask how many people will have been in a position to do all that?"

There was another silence, which Verity was finally willing to break by stating the obvious. "Not many," she said.

"But then," Cecilia continued, "it seems that the doer of all these things is *still* active enough and powerful enough *now* — thirty years later! — to feel threatened when it looks as if the 1986 investigation might re-open, and to arrange the deaths of various people who just possibly once saw something that could assist that investigation. I wonder how many people would fit *that* description as well?"

"Rather fewer," Verity said. "I think you've just created a description of our killer. Or at least, of whoever it is that's behind the killings — the *real* killer."

"Exactly," Cecilia said. "And while I dare say I'm not at all in favour of whatever it is Grimes and Di Stefano and company are up to in the Port of Bristol just at present, that killer is the one I *really* want."

"Just one qualification to that," Verity said.

Cecilia looked at her.

"Although we don't know that Grimes and company are now working for the same person they were working for in 1986, let's not forget that we also don't know that they *aren't*. What's happening at Bristol *might* be another lead to our killer. We just can't tell yet."

"Again, point taken," Cecilia said. "Open minds are the order of the day."

At ten o'clock Ian Salmon, Glyn Davies and Bob Coulter joined them by speakerphone.

The commander had two new pieces of information.

The first was that last night there had been an explosion at Alan Brightman's house in Leadmore Terrace. Brightman himself was away, as Glyn Davies had told him to be, and so were his family. So no one was injured. But the fact of the attack meant that every member of the original black ops team had now been targeted — together, of course, with the detective who had led the original enquiry into Bernard Standish's death.

"Do we know yet if it was the same explosive as the others?"

"Identical. More Russian plastic."

"What about the explosion in Sterling's car?" Cecilia asked.

"They're still working on it. Nothing yet."

The second piece of information was also from London: a report of the autopsy on George Patterson. The details were essentially identical with those for Andrew MacDonald and Charles Soames: a bruised head, signs of an injection under the fingernail, and heightened levels of sodium chloride and chlorine in the body.

"In other words, the same MO in every case," Headley said.

The team next shared the results of their own discussion. Ian Salmon seemed to become quite excited.

"This is excellent," he said after they'd finished. "Between you, you've just drawn a series of conclusions that could be crucial in our getting to the bottom of the murders you're investigating. The National Crime Agency has the resources and authority to check into who might qualify as suspects within the parameters you've discerned. Let's see what they come up with. I shall cogitate and consult."

I do believe he's going to say *the game is afoot*, Cecilia thought. But he didn't. Instead he said, "While all that's happening I think, however, that we have a more immediate task. Just what exactly *are* Grimes and company up to in the Port of Bristol? Given the people involved, I'm perfectly sure it's criminal. As to how it's linked to our murders, I agree with you. That's not clear — as yet. But it will surely become clearer when we've a better idea what it is."

"Apropos which it would be useful to know what's in that container," Tom said. "Preferably before this Di Stefano fellow gets his fingers on it."

"Don't we have grounds for a warrant?" Cecilia said.

"You probably have," Salmon said, "but then the owners would have the right to be present and we'd have an entire performance on our hands that would certainly scare off anyone who mattered."

She nodded. "Point taken."

"Bob Coulter and I were going to go in and take a look last night if the fog hadn't held us up," Davies said. "We can do it tonight. Just a quick in and out! No one needs be any the wiser. Joseph, are we on top of the surveillance?"

"I think so," Joseph said. "Of course you know the Port of Bristol has its own police?"

"We've been watching them," Davies said. "They're pretty sharp, actually. But Bob and I've dealt with sharp people before and we think we have a way to get by them. What else?"

"There are motion sensors and heat sensors in the offices and warehouses. But I don't think you've any reason to be going near them?"

"None whatever. We just want to look in that container."

"Right," Joseph said, "then it's just CCTV cameras, and no problem. I fished around last night and I've managed to find their digital signatures. So tonight at nine fifty-five I can send them a firmware update that'll do no permanent damage but will have them from ten until midnight showing a loop of the previous thirty minutes. It'll look on the monitors as if they've still got coverage, but if you go in during those two hours, nobody will see a thing."

"Perfect."

Joseph Stirrup might be feeling under the weather, Cecilia reflected, but it was still just as well he was on the side of the angels.

TWENTY-TWO

Verity tidied up the last oddments on her desk. It was already dark outside.

Joseph appeared in the doorway, looking a good deal better than he had in the morning. She'd finally persuaded him to take one of his painkillers in the early afternoon and get a couple of hours sleep on the camp bed in his office while one of his staff monitored McConnell's phone. Thank God, it had worked wonders.

But he now stood coatless in the doorway to her office — to her surprise, for they were about to go home.

"Aren't you ready?" she asked. "Where's your jacket?"

He shook his head.

"We've got a problem," he said. "McClintock just took a call from his boss. Di Stefano has decided to change his plans. He's coming across tonight, not Thursday — and it sounds to me as though he and Grimes are planning to descend on the Port of Bristol at exactly the moment the chief super and Bob Coulter are trying to take a surreptitious look at the container."

"Oh my God. You're sure?"

"Listen to it."

He pressed a button on the mobile he was holding, and together they listened.

"I have changed my plans, Signor Grimes. As it happens, neither Thursday nor Friday of this week will now suit me. So I will come this evening and inspect your goods."

"Oh, well, certainly Mr Di Stefano. What time do you expect to arrive?"

"We are about two hours out of Trapani, and my pilot says we will arrive at Bristol Airport at 9.30 p.m. British time. Meet with me at the Royal Portbury Dock at 10.30 at the container. If I am satisfied with what I see, our deal can go through."

"All right then, I'll send a car to meet you at the airport."

"That will not be necessary, Signor Grimes. I have made my own arrangements. My people will drive me to the docks and I will meet you there at the container, as I said."

"Well of course, just as you please. Suit yourself, Mr Di Stefano."

Verity blew out her cheeks when they'd finished listening.

"It sounds to me," she said, "as though Duncan Grimes was rather irritated about Di Stefano making his own transport arrangements—as if he didn't feel trusted."

"I wonder why Di Stefano wouldn't trust him?" Joseph said. "I mean, it's not as if he was a crook or anything, is it?"

She chuckled briefly but then shook her head.

"You're right though," she said. "We do have a problem. Can we get hold of the chief super or Bob Coulter before they go in?"

"First thing I tried. No response."

She nodded. Damn. The chances were they'd already turned everything off so as not to risk a sudden call in the middle of the operation.

This was serious.

"Cecilia?"

"Second thing I did. She's on her way back in. And I've told her I'll stay on here in case they need tech backup that I can't give them from home."

Verity nodded.

"Let's see then. We're able to contact Commander Salmon, aren't we?"

"In an emergency."

"This is definitely an emergency. He needs to know."

A fresh thought struck her.

"Oh my God!"

"Already taken care of," he said, evidently reading her thought. "I called Cecilia's mama. She'll collect Samuel and Hoover from the babysitter and take them over to the rectory for tonight."

Samuel was their one-year old son, and Hoover their wriggling, adoring dog.

Verity stared at him.

"I anticipated," he said.

"You definitely have your moments, Joseph Stirrup!"

He grinned.

"I know."

She laughed and hugged him. Given the situation that had just arisen, her timing was perhaps rather odd, but the fact was she felt deliciously happy. She'd always loved his beautiful smile, and especially she loved it now when it told her he was feeling better.

So what if a difficulty had arisen? They'd solve the problem somehow.

In main reception PC Brenda Cosgrove was talking with Sergeant Stillwell. Obviously, she'd just come off duty. She looked anxiously at Verity, and after a moment's hesitation said, "Ma'am?"

"Yes, Brenda?"

"Is there… I mean, I'll understand if you can't say… but I just wondered, is everything all right?"

Verity stared at her. Throughout the time since Bob Coulter went under cover the young woman had been a model of discretion and patience, never once asking questions or querying anything that was going on. So just what was it that caused her to ask precisely this question at this moment?

"I think I'll just go and make sure that those… that those other things are all right," Sergeant Stillwell said, and walked off.

Verity hesitated only a moment. She knew exactly how she would feel if it were Joseph out on the line. And Brenda Cosgrove was a good officer. She deserved a response.

"Just between us, Brenda."

"Understood ma'am."

"Bob was fine when we last spoke with him, which was at about ten-thirty this morning. Since then, a situation's arisen that we didn't expect — a situation that could be dangerous. But we're onto it, and we're doing our absolute best to make sure everyone's okay. And as you know, Bob is in any case pretty good at taking care of himself."

Brenda smiled. "I know that ma'am. And thank you — thank you for being straight with me."

Verity nodded. It was, she reflected, the least that she could do — that, and pray to God that Bob and the chief super did indeed come out of this all right.

TWENTY-THREE

Bristol, Royal Portbury Docks,
Alberta Quay, Berth 2,
in the General Products Terminal.
Later that evening.

G lyn Davies and Bob Coulter used a covert ops trick that had worked for them a couple of times in their former lives, and entered the terminal surreptitiously at about ten-thirty.

It wasn't until they were successfully in that Davies found himself muttering, "Bob, I'm think getting a bit old for this!"

Coulter merely chuckled. "You're doing fine, sir."

Thanks to CMS Streetwise lighting, visibility on the dock was quite good, though Davies found the result somewhat eerie. No doubt the place was busy enough during the day, but at night there were just silent lines of containers representing, he supposed, millions of pounds' worth of wealth from every corner of the earth, while over them loomed the gantry cranes, three of them, stark and massive against the night sky. Everywhere there were CCTV cameras, all of them, he trusted, thanks to Joseph now lying cheerfully to those who monitored them.

Following a plan of the docks on Davies' phone, also provided by Joseph, they were able among the hundreds of containers to find without difficulty the one that interested them. Then they had another wait, ten minutes or so, until the officers patrolling the port passed this section. They had earlier worked out that the patrols came by every thirty minutes, which meant that if they allowed themselves twenty-nine minutes to inspect the container and leave, they would have one minute to spare.

The patrol passed: and then, for a moment, when they got to the container and examined it, Davies was taken aback.

"Damn it!" he whispered. "It's got one of those new finger print scanners. Can you do anything with that?"

"I don't know, sir. You see the real problem would be the retinal scanner."

"There's a retinal scanner, too? For God's sake!"

Bob Coulter chuckled again.

"Just kidding."

Davies shook his head. "All right. You got me. But you can do something with the finger print scanner?"

"Let's see, shall we?"

Bob Coulter produced from his knapsack various small items.

"The fact is," he whispered as he worked, "finger print scanners have mostly made breaking and entering easier. Ninety-nine people out a hundred don't bother to *wipe* the thing after using it. Which means almost always there's a fingerprint left on it. So then, with a little magnetic powder," — he dusted the scanner — "and the right sticky tape... like that... you can lift the print and the chances are" — he did some things with the tape and applied the result to the scanner — "it will turn out to be just the print you needed."

There was a click and an orange light on the lock turned green.

"Voilà!" he said.

Davies looked at his watch. So far they'd used seven of their minutes.

"Brilliant," he said. "Okay, let's see what we've got."

The doors were smooth, and opened without a din. That took them another minute, though.

They peered inside.

"Good God Almighty!"

"Bloody hell!"

What faced them was neither surplus weaponry nor a collection of stolen artefacts. It was cash, a mountain of it: neat oblong shrink-wrapped packages of American one hundred dollar bills, rising from floor to ceiling.

"It's got to be counterfeit."

Davies eased one package out and peered at it, then broke the seal and ruffled through it. "No," he said, looking closely at it, "I don't think it is. I'm pretty sure these are genuine one hundred dollar bills. No wonder Lucio Di Stefano is interested. If I'm right this is a money launderer's dream."

"Where the hell did it all come from?"

"Iraq, for certain... as the manifest said. After the 2003 invasion the Americans flew nearly twelve billion dollars in cash into Iraq for reconstruction. Billions of it went missing. And a good deal of it's here or I'm a Dutchman."

"Good analysis," a voice came from behind them, accompanied by a soft, slow handclap, "very good indeed. Pity you've no business being here."

Davies whipped round as suddenly they found themselves surrounded: eight men, who within seconds produced handguns and covered them. Mitch McConnell, Duncan Grimes' sidekick, was one of them.

He sensed Bob Coulter beside him tense for a moment, and then relax muttering, "Too many." He nodded. Coulter was good, but even he couldn't take out eight armed men who had the drop on them.

And now Duncan Grimes, who had spoken, became visible at the back of the group.

They were presumably here to inspect their container—as expected.

Only they were here three days early—as *not* expected.

But what about the CCTV cameras? They weren't working, but Duncan Grimes didn't know that, did he? How did he dare risk this confrontation in front of them? Davies glanced up, and realized at once why Grimes had dared. There were two cameras that might have covered the scene—and both were obviously damaged. His glance had, however, revealed his thought, or part of it.

"I don't think the CCTV will help you," Grimes said. "One of my lads took those out half an hour ago. I didn't want some nosey Port officer spotting what we had in here when we opened up the crate. So—a couple of well-aimed rocks! Easy! This is now officially a blind spot."

Crude, compared to Joseph, but effective. Damn! There were guidelines for covert operations and he'd just blown one of the most basic: be alert for anything out of the ordinary. He should have spotted those damaged cameras and been on his guard.

"The Port Police are pretty efficient, mind you," Grimes was continuing. "I dare say they'll have them fixed first thing tomorrow. But that's not going to help you now, is it? So—as I said, a good analysis. And clever of you to have broken into the container. Unfortunately for you, too clever for your own good. I don't know who you are, and I don't care. You're out of your depth and you're in our way. There's too much at stake here to mess around. McConnell, do your job. Shoot them and then dump the bodies in the dock."

Why McConnell?

Oh yes, he could see why.

McConnell's gun was fitted with a silencer.

TWENTY-FOUR

The same, seconds later.

G lyn Davies looked at Bob Coulter out of the corner of his eye.

Coulter gave a faint smile and an even fainter shrug.

Davies sighed. Another guideline for covert ops was to avoid notice. Blend in with the scenery. A natural corollary of that was to avoid getting into fights, and especially fights you couldn't win. If you were faced with a fight you couldn't win you should definitely run away from it.

But what if you couldn't even do that?

Stall.

"I think," he said, "that you would be very unwise not to talk to us before you have us killed."

"And why would that be?"

Good question. What lie might be interesting and surprising enough to slow Grimes down?

"Look," he said, "we both know who you take your orders from."

Which was all he could think of, but was a lot to hang on Cecilia's speculations and a four second phone call.

"And what about him?"

Davies barely prevented himself from whistling. So there *was* someone—a man—giving orders! This was progress—assuming of course that he and Bob Coulter ever got out of here to share it with anyone.

"Well," Davies said, "let's just say he gives us our orders too. Why do you think we're here?"

When one couldn't think of a single valid reason why one was in an impossible position, always try giving the other side a chance to come up with its own fantasy. They might be better at it than you.

"Rubbish."

A strong word... but there'd been a slight hesitation. Grimes wasn't *quite* sure, was he? A seed of doubt had been sown.

"If that's really what you think," Davies said, "then I suggest you call him. Tell him you're just about to execute his west of England agents. Let's see how that works for you, Mr Grimes."

This was, he hoped, the right moment to show that he knew Grimes' name even though Grimes didn't know his.

Still, quite what would have happened if Grimes had actually accepted his suggestion and made the call he was destined never to find out: for at that moment all of them were bathed in bright beams of light that swept round from behind and somewhat to the left of him and Bob Coulter to shine full in the faces of Grimes and his men.

Now what?

He could hear tires on tarmac pulling up behind him beside the container... a car engine... no, two car engines... soft and powerful... the soft click of car doors... the sharp click of high heels ... and a woman's voice, speaking English but with a heavy Italian accent. She didn't shout but she spoke as one in authority who had no need to speak quietly—as one who had dealt with security and come in through the front gate.

"Signor Duncan Grimes?"

That was odd. Surely he knew that voice?

"That's me," Grimes said, "and who are you?"

"I am Giuseppina Di Stefano, granddaughter of Lucio Di Stefano. I am here on behalf of my grandfather."

"Oh, I'd understood Mr Di Stefano would be coming —"

"My grandfather was somewhat indisposed after the flight and has remained on our aircraft. So now you will speak with me."

"Well of course, Miss Di Stefano, but if —"

"And already, Signor Grimes, I am not pleased with this scene. My father understood that you wished to do business with us, not produce a drama."

Surely he knew that voice?

"This is merely an unexpected hiccup, which I assure you —"

"Signor Grimes, it does not matter to me how you deal with your domestic problems. But if you wish to do business with *la famiglia Di Stefano*, you will not deal with those problems in front of me. *Se minacci la gente non fai altro che metterti nei guai.* It does not please me to be... *come si dice?*... an accessory to murder."

She had walked forward and was now in Davies' line of vision. Tall, elegant, long dark hair, dark fashion glasses, a full-length fur coat — surely sable? — and high-heeled *stivali da donna*.

As God was his judge, it was Cecilia Cavaliere, and he'd be damned if she wasn't enjoying every minute of this.

Behind her, two young men in dark suits with dark glasses, arms folded, suitably expressionless.

Detective Constables Tom Wilkins and Headley Jarman.

And behind them he could see out of the corner of his eye two gleaming silver Mercedes Maybach S600 Pullman limousines, lights still on, engines running.

"My apologies, Miss Di Stefano," Grimes said, evidently impressed by this parade of panache. "McClintock, have some of your people take... our guests back to the ship. We can deal with them later."

McClintock nodded to a couple of his men, who came up to Davies and Coulter, jabbed them with their guns, and said, "Move."

They moved.

"And do persuade the rest of your fellows to put away all those guns, Signor Grimes," he heard Cecilia saying as they left. "It is not civilized. And in your country, I believe, it is not even legal."

As, of course, it wasn't. With very few exceptions handguns had been illegal for private ownership in the United Kingdom since 1997. But still... to point that out in this situation! Glyn Davies only just avoided shaking his head in disbelief. Had Cecilia Cavaliere got some nerve, or had she got some nerve?

They were directed by their captors to walk along the line of parked containers, then to turn right, out of sight (presumably) of the group gathered round the container with the money. They then proceeded along another line of containers toward the dock and (presumably) *La Luna Rossa*.

"There aren't too many now!" Bob Coulter said to no one in particular as they walked.

"No talking," said one of their captors, and jabbed him in the shoulder blades.

"Let's go a bit further," Davies said, "'til we're out of earshot."

"Right you are."

"*No* talking!" — and another jab.

They walked on.

"You know the problem with handguns?" Coulter said after they'd covered another thirty yards or so.

"I *said* no talk!" his captor said, again jabbing him viciously in the back — at which point, as more than once in the past, what Bob Coulter did was almost too fast for Davies to follow. In a single movement he pivoted, seized his captor's handgun, twisted it out of his hand, and sent him reeling with a head butt. Then as his colleague turned from covering Davies, Coulter tossed the handgun hard into his face, twisted *his* gun out of his hand, and kneed him in the groin.

He made some effort to fight back, as did his colleague, but they were both now groggy, and Coulter knocked them unconscious without apparent difficulty.

"The problem with handguns," he said softly as he looked down at the prone figures, "is that most people using them tend to get too close to the target. And then if you're the target they're just a doddle to disarm."

He picked up the two pistols and ejected the magazines, then threw the magazines in one direction and the guns in another.

"Makarov PMs," he said as he did so. "They're pretty good weapons, actually... standard Russian police issue since the fifties... though in the west, getting the right ammo for them can sometimes be a bit of a problem. Still, they definitely deserve better than those two clowns. So what now, boss?"

Abruptly, his tone changed and he grinned, though still he spoke softly.

"Here's DI Jones, sir—with the cavalry, I think. Good evening, ma'am."

Flanked by several armed police officers, Verity Jones had emerged from behind the line of containers facing them.

"'Evening, Bob. We were *supposed* to be the cavalry," she said, matching his quiet tone, "but it looks as though you don't need us."

"We may yet," Davies said. "I take it you know what our friend Cecilia is up to?"

"Yes sir. Long story for later. It was mostly Commander Salmon who fixed everything. He's in the second limo, but he's keeping a low profile. Detective Superintendent Cavaliere's wired, so we're hoping this time to get the real goods on Grimes."

"Right. Well first have your people make sure that when those two wake up they're well cuffed to a container."

Verity nodded to a couple of the armed officers, who went to Bob Coulter's two still unconscious adversaries and secured them.

"Good," Davies said. "Now let's return discreetly to the negotiations, and see how Our Woman On The Inside is faring."

TWENTY-FIVE

The Royal Portsbury Dock, the quay, by the container.
About the same time.

When Grimes' men threw back the container doors and revealed the wall of dollar bills Cecilia was, she had to admit to herself, somewhat taken aback. She had never before in her life seen so much money.

"There you are," Grimes said. "Reconstruction money from Iraq. Good, wholesome American bills, straight from the United States Treasury. *Three* billion dollars' worth of them! That container is full to the far end."

Impressive.

But she'd so far held the initiative in this conversation and she was determined to keep it. Grimes had emphasized "three". Either that meant there was more here than might have been expected or there was less. His manner, however, was self-satisfied. Which surely meant that there was more. He expected her to be impressed.

"That is more than was discussed," she said in her iciest tones.

"That's so. We were even more successful than we expected. Is that a problem for you?"

She walked towards him, gazed down at him, and then shook her head.

"The more money, the more risk, Signor Grimes. That is elementary. I would have expected you to know this."

He frowned.

"All right, so there's more here than you expected," he said. "Rome wasn't built in a day. Just take it slowly. Is your father up to the job or not? Perhaps he's getting too old for it?"

She gave him her most scornful look.

"The point at issue, Signor Grimes, is not my father's competence. The point at issue is — there are rules for such transactions as these, and you do not seem to know what they are. I do not like dealing with amateurs."

His mouth tightened. She was getting to him. He didn't like her lecturing him in front of his men.

"Do you think I've never done this kind of thing before?" he said.

"It is certainly starting to look like it."

She was now standing close to him, and she could see his eyes bulge and his face darken. He was furious. He would like to have struck her. For the second time in days she found herself thinking of Jane Austen's words—"angry people are not always wise." Perhaps this was the moment to test that.

"Tell me, Signor Grimes," she said quietly, but still not so quietly that his men would not hear her, "given the changes you have made from what was originally discussed, what exactly do you now want from my father?"

He made a visible effort to control himself.

"Simply," he said, "to handle these dollar bills, *as was originally discussed*. Do I have to spell it out? Obtaining this money, getting it here from Iraq, it's been a complex and risky business. We've done our part. All I expect of your father is to use his resources to get these notes into the legal bank accounts and businesses we specified so that their origin can't be traced. And to do so, incidentally, for a very handsome fee—as was also originally discussed. Now, is that clear enough for you?"

"Quite clear enough!" came Commander Salmon's voice in her earbud. "That's exactly what we need, Detective Superintendent Cavaliere! Arrest him."

As Salmon spoke, lights came on, presumably at his instigation, flooding the area.

Out of nowhere, it seemed, armed police surrounded them. Verity Jones, accompanied by Glyn Davies and Bob Coulter, emerged from the darkness.

"What—?" Grimes looked around him in amazement.

"I am Detective Superintendent Cecilia Cavaliere, Exeter CID," Cecilia said in her normal English voice. "Duncan Grimes, I'm arresting you for being in possession of stolen currency, and for attempting to smuggle it into or by way of the United Kingdom. You do not have to say anything, but it may harm your defence if you fail to mention when questioned something which you intend to rely on in court. Anything you do say may be given in evidence. Do you understand this?"

He stared at her open mouthed.

"In other words, you're nicked," she said. "Cuff him, DI Jones."

"Ma'am."

"And then have your officers arrest all the others, will you? They were all waving handguns when I arrived, which was, as I pointed out to them at the time, in itself an illegal act, so for now we can confiscate those and charge them with illegal possession. We can get to other charges later. Also, this container is a crime scene. We need to tape it off."

"On it, ma'am."

Verity gave instructions to various uniformed officers, who began the work.

"Don't forget there are also a couple of them back there on the quay handcuffed to a container," Bob Coulter said. "And their guns—two Makarov PMs and their magazines—are also somewhere on the ground near where you met us, DI Jones."

Verity chuckled. "So they are! Coulson, Hicks, Carlson, go and find them!"

"Ma'am."

Three of the officers went to look.

"They'll probably still be asleep," Coulter called after them as they were leaving. "Try to be gentle when you wake them up!"

"So Signor Grimes," Cecilia said, approaching him and dropping again into her Italian accent, "you were right. Rome was not built in a day." She smiled, and switched to her usual voice. "But it burned in a night! And that, in case you're interested, was the eighteenth of July, AD 64: which became for the Romans much what I suspect tonight will become for you—a night to remember."

TWENTY-SIX

Bristol, the Royal Portbury Dock.
About half an hour later.

"Oh, my part was easy," Commander Salmon said with a dismissive wave of the hand. "Nothing at all compared to the adventures the rest of you have been having."

They—Commander Salmon, Glyn Davies, Cecilia, Verity, Bob Coulter, Headley and Tom—were gathered in an office in the Port of Bristol Police Headquarters at the Royal Portsbury Dock, debriefing and sharing information after the night's adventures. All of them, Cecilia thought, including even the commander, were somewhat high after what had happened, eager to hear each other's stories and understand how it had all played out.

"By the way, Detective Superintendent Cavaliere," Salmon continued, "I feel I should apologize for bringing you here in a mere Mercedes. It was what Lucio Di Stefano's own people had hired, and I didn't think I should change it. Personally, I'd have tried to find you something Italian."

Cecilia smiled. "That's quite all right, sir. Given a fur coat by Paolo Moretti, boots by Sergio Rossi—they are utterly gorgeous incidentally!—and sunglasses by Dolce e Gabbana, I definitely had no problem with a short ride in a German car!"

Being a well-brought-up young woman, she normally didn't approve of using real fur for fashion, and in her own wardrobe dutifully insisted on *pelliccia ecologica*. But as she'd just admitted in a quiet aside to Verity, she couldn't deny that sable did make a most gorgeous coat, and while wearing it she felt like a millionaire.

"Which," as the ever-realistic Verity pointed out, "you'd need to be if you were going to own one!"

As for the car —

"German or not, it's a magnificent car," Tom said. "You can't deny that."

Cecilia nodded. "To tell the truth, sir, I don't know how you arranged it all in the time you had."

"It was easy enough," Salmon said. "Petty well all I had to do was wander about giving orders."

"But didn't you have to deal with Di Stefano, sir — the Mafia man?" Verity said.

"I did. But it wasn't difficult."

"Can we know about it?"

"Well, from the moment we learnt that Lucio Di Stefano was going to meet with Grimes, it occurred to me how much more likely we'd be to catch Grimes out in some really damaging admission if we could persuade Di Stefano to miss the appointment and have someone of our own — someone wired — meet him instead. And the fact that we actually had in Detective Superintendent Cavaliere someone who could be an entirely convincing Mafiosa seemed altogether too good an opportunity to miss. So — how could we persuade Di Stefano to miss his appointment? That was the only question. Hard approach or soft? For better or worse I decided on soft. My plans were coming together nicely when I learnt from Mr Stirrup that Di Stefano had changed his plans and was arriving tonight instead of later in the week! So we had to bring the operation forward. But it was no real problem. I arranged for Di Stefano's plane to be held in an area by the runway when he landed, then had myself driven out there and boarded it."

"I don't imagine he was very pleased with that," Headley said.

"Not at first. But then overall I think the meeting went well. I welcomed him to the United Kingdom and, having previously been briefed on his taste for fine cognac, presented him with a bottle of Croizet Cuvée Léonie Exclusive as a token of our good will."

Bob Coulter whistled.

"That," he said, "was serious good will."

Ian Salmon smiled. "I then went on to explain to him that he had a choice. As a free citizen of the European Union, of which the United Kingdom was at present still part, and as one who had, so far as I knew, committed no crimes in the United Kingdom, he was of course entirely free if he chose to enter the country and go about whatever business he had planned for the evening. If he did that, however, I could not answer for the consequences, and especially not if that business had anything to do with the Royal Portbury Dock, which I rather thought might this evening be the focus of some police attention."

There were chuckles at this, which Salmon acknowledged with a half smile.

"Alternatively," he continued, "Signor Di Stefano could without more ado order his plane to take off immediately and return to Sicily, knowing that if he did so he would leave Britain as one considered by the Secret Intelligence Service to have rendered valuable assistance in an important operation. I took the liberty of adding that his flight's communications would be monitored during this return flight, and any attempt to communicate with anyone other than air traffic control would not be viewed favourably. Such monitoring, I explained, was mandated by the SIS in situations such as this, though in the present case I regarded it as unnecessary since I was sure that as a man of honour he wouldn't dream of attempting such communication."

He paused for a moment.

"Faced with this choice," he continued, "and being evidently a man of good sense, Signor Di Stefano accepted the cognac graciously and assured me that being a monarchist at heart and in particular a lifelong admirer of Her Majesty, he would always be happy to oblige any agent of the Crown. I imagine that by now he is well on his way back to Trapani, if not already arrived."

He paused for a moment, and then said to Cecilia and Verity, "Since Grimes and his people have been arrested for crimes in Bristol, they're being transferred to the formal custody of the Avon and Somerset Constabulary, as is also control of the crime scene. But I've arranged for you two to interview Grimes on behalf of Exeter CID tomorrow morning at Bridewell Street Police Station. Let's see if you can get anything out of him apropos the particular cases that interest you."

"Thank you, sir," Cecilia said. "Do you think maybe I ought to wear those Sergio Rossi boots and the fur coat again? They might throw him off his stride, don't you think?"

He laughed. "They evidently devastated him earlier this evening! Alas, they're already on their way back to the agency we borrowed them from. But fear not! I am utterly confident in your and Detective Inspector Jones' ability to throw him off his stride even without those accoutrements!"

He turned to Davies.

"Glyn, you and I *won't* be involved in those interviews — though I dare say we may discreetly watch — because I'm determined we shall continue to be out of the picture. Almost no one but the people in this room knows we haven't been assassinated and I'm anxious to keep it that way. I want whoever Mr Big is to think that even though he's lost the Iraqi money he's succeeded in eliminating all the original witnesses from the 1986 black bag op. Understood?"

Everyone nodded.

"By the way," he said, "Cavaliere—I do have a question. Your performance this evening as Signorina Di Stefano was every bit as dazzling as I expected. But one thing about it puzzles me. How did you know that three billion dollars was more than Grimes had discussed with her father?"

Cecilia gave a half smile and shook her head. "I didn't sir. It was just a lucky guess."

He stared at her.

"It was the expression on his face," she said, "and the way he emphasized 'three' when he showed me the money. I felt sure he was saying, 'Look, aren't I a clever boy! There's more here than you expected!' So I decided I'd play on that by disappointing him. That seemed to irritate him—which was what I wanted."

"Which led him to give you an angry lecture on what he wanted from the Di Stefanos, which was exactly what *I* wanted." Ian Salmon nodded. "Perfect."

"Do you know what's going to happen to all that money, sir?" Verity asked after another moment or so of silence.

"Ah yes, the money. Since at least two foreign governments are involved, that, I imagine, will be something for the Foreign Office to sort out."

"You don't think maybe as finders we ought to get half?" she said. "Split it up between us?"

There was a general chuckle, including from Commander Salmon.

"An excellent idea, Detective Inspector Jones! I shall certainly see that it's passed on to the Foreign Office. As the man in charge I shall naturally, of course, expect a larger slice than the rest of you!"

"That seems fair, sir."

There was another pause.

Somebody smothered a yawn.

It was suddenly evident that, as the adrenalin settled and immediate curiosity was satisfied, everyone was starting to flag. Salmon himself, Cecilia thought, looked very tired.

He gave another half smile.

"It's been a long day and a long night. Again, excellent work by everyone, but we need some rest. The NCA has booked accommodations for us at Winston Manor, which I think you'll find acceptable. Those wonderful German limousines can take us there."

No one made any objection to that.

"I take it that brandy—what was it? Croizet Cuvée Léonie—is rather special?" Verity said to Bob Coulter as she and Cecilia were walking back with him to the limousines.

He laughed. "You could say that, ma'am. Naturally it'll depend on the year, but a bottle of 1858 was sold at auction a few years back for $156,000."

"Crikey! How on earth could you bring yourself to drink something that expensive? About a thousand dollars a nip!"

"I suppose," he said, "it'd be sort of like travelling back in time. You'd be drinking something that predated phylloxera."

"I would? And what's that?" Verity said.

"It was an epidemic—an insect from North America that very nearly wiped out the French wine industry in the 1860s. The eventual cure for it—well, it wasn't exactly a cure—was to graft the European vines onto resistant American rootstock. But there are those who claim that though it worked and meant wine growing could more or less get back to normal, it produced wine that isn't as good."

"My goodness, how on earth do you know all this?" Verity said.

"I find it interesting, and I like to know about what I'm drinking." He chuckled. "Anyway, it makes a nice change from guns."

"At that price I still think I'd get indigestion just thinking about it," Cecilia said.

"Well, ma'am," he said, "if it makes you feel better, I'm sure that what they gave Di Stefano wasn't an 1858 or anything like it. But even if it was, what's $156,000 when it turns out we were playing for three billion?"

TWENTY-SEVEN

Monday, 26ᵗʰ September.
Bristol, Bridewell Street Police Station.

When Cecilia and Verity entered the interview room at
Bridewell Street Police Station the following morning,
Duncan Grimes and his solicitor were already there. Grimes had,
so Cecilia understood, been questioned earlier and at length by
the Somerset and Avon police. Nevertheless she began their own
part of the proceedings, as was her custom, by reminding him
why they were being recorded and cautioning him that his rights
and responsibilities remained exactly as they had no doubt been
explained to him earlier.

"Yes, yes, I understand all that," he said.

She looked at his solicitor, who nodded acquiescence.

"Good. Now Detective Inspector Jones and I only want to talk
with you about one thing. Last night in the course of your conversation at the Royal Portbury Dock before my arrival, the man you
had cornered said, and I quote, 'We all know who you take your
orders from,' and you replied, 'And what about him?' Is that a
correct record of what happened?"

"It may be."

"Either you think it's correct or you don't, Mr Grimes."

He looked at his solicitor, who shook his head.

"Is it correct?"

"I don't remember."

"I really find that hard to believe. It was a dramatic moment. Plenty of other people were around you at the time, and they seem to remember quite well, including several of your own men, who are now in custody and being questioned. No doubt they'll tell their own stories."

He shrugged.

"All I want from you," Cecilia said, "is to answer your own question, 'What about him?' Tell me about the man you get your orders from."

"I've nothing to say."

"Well, perhaps not. But tell me," — she produced from the file in front of her a sheet of paper with a number on it and slid it across for him to see — "if I call that telephone number, who will answer?"

It was the mysterious number that had called McClintock for four seconds.

Grimes looked at it and glanced away — rather too quickly.

"Never seen it in my life before."

"O now *really*, Mr Grimes!" she said, smiling and shaking her head. "That's *terribly* unconvincing."

She sat back in her chair and looked at him.

"So," she continued after a moment, "if you've never seen that number in your life before, why would you have been receiving calls from it and making calls to it?"

"My client doesn't adm—" his solicitor started to say, but Grimes brushed his intervention aside angrily.

"Bugger that! Christ, you people have been tapping my phones!"

Cecilia looked at Verity, who laughed and shook her head as she took up the questioning.

"No Mr Grimes, you weren't *listening* to my colleague. Her question was very carefully phrased so as to be *hypothetical*. Actually, we haven't tapped your phones. But what *you've* just done is tell us that if we *had*, we'd have heard you calling and being called from a number you just said you'd never seen in your life before."

Verity paused, giving time for this to sink in.

"Jesus Christ!" Grimes said. "You don't look like a complete bitch."

"So people tell me," she said. "Anyway, let me repeat Superintendent Cavaliere's question. If I called the number she's just shown you, who would answer? Or, since we already both know the answer to that question, we could skip it and get straight back to the original question, the *real* question—what about the man you take your orders from? Tell us about him."

Grimes looked at his solicitor, who shrugged with a "You-wouldn't-shut-up-when-I-was-trying-to-tell-you-to, so-now-what-do-you-expect-me-to-do?" expression on his face.

"Listen, Mr Grimes," Verity said, "you surely know that Somerset and Avon Police have you dead to rights on some very serious charges. You were caught red-handed in the docks last night with billions of pounds' worth of stolen foreign currency. And now you've as good as admitted you're in phone contact with someone who's of great interest to us. What we're asking can't possibly make matters any worse for you. But if you're co-operative, they might make them a little better."

She sat back and waited while he conferred in a whisper with the lawyer.

"All right," he said abruptly, turning back to her. "Have it your way. The fact is, I don't *know* anything much about him. That's the truth."

"But you talk to him," Cecilia said.

"By phone. He gives me a phone number, and I call it, or he calls me. Every few months, he changes the number. Now and then he gives me instructions and I carry them out. And then money appears in my bank account. I can't even tell where it's come from. That's all I know. And it's been like that for years."

"How many years?"

"Christ, I don't know. Years! Look, I'm not admitting to anything else."

"That's all right, I'm not trying to get you to. But let's see," – Cecilia looked at a note in her folder–"I see you were charged with selling smuggled weapons in 1985 – "

"Christ, don't you people ever forget? I was acquitted on that."

"Of course you were, all fair and above board! Don't get your knickers in a twist! All I'm trying to do is jog your memory. Could you have been talking occasionally to this man as long ago as that?"

Grimes looked at his solicitor, who looked at Cecilia.

"You're not questioning the verdict, then?" the solicitor said.

"Absolutely not! Your client was innocent! Pure as the driven snow! Anything you like! All I'm trying to do is to find out how long he's known this fellow. Did he know him back then?"

The solicitor looked at Grimes and nodded.

"All right, maybe I did. I was a young bloke when he first linked up with me."

That was what she really wanted to find out. Anything else would be icing on the cake. She looked at Verity.

"What does this man sound like when he talks to you?" Verity said, stepping in on her cue.

"Posh," he said after a moment's consideration. "A bit like you two, but even posher."

"So what do you talk about? What kinds of instructions does he give you?"

"He gets me to move things round for him."

"What things?"

He said nothing.

"Well," Verity said, "we know at least one answer to that, don't we? Last night, as you admitted on the docks—and don't forget we have in evidence a recording of you saying this—you were moving those millions of pounds worth of stolen foreign currency we just mentioned so they could be laundered by Impresa Gabriella—that's to say by the Italian Mafia. And the Mafia—doubtless after taking their own percentage—were to get it as clean money into legal bank accounts and businesses, some of which, I dare say, belong to your posh friend on the phone."

Grimes shrugged.

"Do you and this person on the phone talk about anything *other* than your moving things for him?"

"I don't know what you mean."

"The point is," Cecilia said, "my colleague and I aren't so much interested in this money-laundering business as in several murders in which your posh friend may be implicated. So if you know something about those and don't tell us, you could find yourself being charged as an accessory to murder."

"Not to mention conspiring to pervert the course of justice," Verity added.

"Yes, of course," Cecilia said. "There'd be that too."

"I don't know about any murders," Grimes said. "He's never told me to kill anyone. Like I told you, I just move things around for him. That's all."

Cecilia raised an eyebrow and gazed at him. He gazed back. On this at least she inclined, overall, to believe him. They'd seen last night how he operated. Certainly he was a murderous thug who would blast out of his way anyone who was in it. But she didn't think he was a hit man.

She looked at Verity, who shook her head. "I've no more questions, ma'am."

"Right." Cecilia got to her feet, gathering her papers as she did so. "Then thank you, Mr Grimes." She nodded to his solicitor, and glanced at the clock on the wall by the door. "Interview terminated at 10.17 a.m.," she added for the benefit of the recording.

Outside the interview room Salmon and Davies met them. Salmon was smiling broadly.

"There you are," he said, "didn't I say you'd be quite capable of throwing him off his stride without the fur coat!"

Cecilia smiled. "Thank you, sir."

"Now then," he said, "what have we got? You've confirmed that we have a phone number connected with the man he takes his orders from, and that it's attached to a disposable prepaid phone that will no doubt be changed shortly — what I understand our American friends call 'a burner.' You've also learnt two new things — that he's been taking orders from this fellow for a very long time, apparently as long ago as 1985, and that whoever he is, he's 'posh', at least by Duncan Grimes' standards — even 'posher' than you two! All that's useful information. All in all, a *very* profitable half hour."

He paused, and took a deep breath. Despite his cheerful manner, Cecilia did not think he looked at all well.

After a moment he continued, "I told you I think the NCA can help with this business, and we can. It's going to take my researchers a few days to complete our enquiries, some of which are going to be rather delicate. So I rather think nothing much will be happening for a few days. Give us a week. Then I should have something concrete to contribute. It's about time. You people have done all the work so far."

Given his last minute organization of things at the Royal Portbury last night, Cecilia thought that he was being somewhat hard on himself, but she said nothing.

TWENTY-EIGHT

During the week that followed the events in Bristol there were, as Ian Salmon predicted, few in the way of apparent developments. Joseph used the list of Charlie Soames' old army friends as provided by his wife to set up video links, and Cecilia and Verity interviewed them, but without learning much that they did not already know. As Salmon had requested, the chief super remained out of sight, and for the day-to-day running of the Heavitree Police Station the Chief Constable sent a temporary replacement.

Apart from those details, it seemed to Cecilia that life pretty well returned to its usual rhythms.

Her "late morning" went back to being properly late, and people were able to finish their boiled eggs and toast and marmalade in peace.

"Serious crime" was again what it generally was in Exeter, for the most part a matter of thefts and frauds, with one case of murder whose rather pathetic perpetrator was identified and apprehended without much difficulty.

PC Brenda Cosgrove was once more her usual bubbly self. Cecilia, having twice seen her sitting in the canteen with Bob Coulter, the two of them evidently well content with each other's company, was left wondering how on earth she could have missed what had apparently been perfectly obvious to everyone else for some time.

And the weather was dreadful—by turns wet and blustery and hot and humid, such, as Jane Austen might have put it, as to keep one in a continual state of inelegance. Even DI Verity Jones arrived at the station on one or two mornings looking very slightly dishevelled.

Charlie Soames' funeral was in St. Bede's Church at eleven o'clock on Tuesday morning, with the committal following it at the Exeter and Devon Crematorium. There was, as Michael expected, a good turnout, including Cecilia and Verity and Joseph.

Michael preached.

As was his practice at funerals where the circumstances of death were notably disturbing or tragic, he touched on the bitterness of life. "We are surrounded," he said, "by a constant alternation of love and hate, truth and falsehood, wisdom and folly, order and disorder, cooperation and sabotage, truth and falsehood, in which the presence of a loving God is by no means always either discernable or even imaginable. We live in endless negotiation with a reality that at times seems not so much implacable as simply meaningless."

Those, he continued, who felt God's absence amid all this were surely at one with our Lord, who cried out as he hung upon the cross, "My God, my God, why have you forsaken me?"

And yet there remained the paradox: that those various pairs—love and hate, truth and falsehood—though opposite were by no means equal. For while it was entirely possible to imagine a universe in which there was neither hate, nor falsehood, nor disorder, a universe where all things worked together, it was quite *impossible* to imagine a universe *without* love or truth or order, a universe in which nothing worked together. As a friend of his had recently pointed out, even piracy requires collaboration. A universe *without* truth or order or cooperation would simply be chaos, *tohu vebohu*, without form and void, just such as the ancient Hebrews envisaged the world until God's Spirit moved on the face of the waters. And was not this ultimate pre-eminence of love, truth and cooperation in itself some cause for hope?

And then for Christians in particular there was the mystery of the third day, with its call to see through and beyond the bitterness of death to a new possibility: the resurrection of the dead. "Christ is risen!" "He is risen indeed!"

What, if Saint Paul was right, that there is indeed a glory to be revealed in us that shall outweigh all present suffering?

What if Gustav Mahler was right?

"O glaube, mein Herz, o glaube:

"Es geht dir nichts verloren!"

"O believe, my heart, O believe:

"Nothing to you is lost!"

"It is in this hope," Michael concluded, "that we pray for Charlie Soames, and for all the departed, that they may rest in peace and rise in glory."

As for the singing, that went quite well, which just showed, as Michael said afterwards, "that people can manage perfectly well with the good stuff if you just give them a chance." The reception in the village hall was well attended and there, as he hoped, people were able to reminisce and celebrate Charlie Soames, his quirks and foibles, his kindness and his sense of fun, to their hearts' content. Most important of all, as far has he was concerned, Enid Soames seemed content with it all, or at least as content as was possible.

Cecilia had one conversation at the reception that she found especially moving. It was with one of Charlie's old army friends, a retired major of the Cheshire Regiment who'd served with him in
Bosnia as part of the U.N. peacekeeping force.

"But I thought Charlie was with the Devon and Dorset Regiment," she said.

"Indeed he was," said the other. "But he'd volunteered to do a
tour with us as Battalion Intelligence Officer since we were a little
under strength in that department. And he was damned good."

"I've been told he always really wanted to be a teacher."

He nodded. "That's true—but don't misunderstand it. Charlie
made no secret that when his SSC was up he wouldn't be applying to extend it but was going to train as a schoolmaster. And
from all we're hearing about him this morning he was obviously a
fine one—which doesn't surprise me at all. In my experience he
was a man who put his heart and soul into whatever he was doing. But that also meant that so long as he was a soldier he was a
soldier and as I said, a damned good one. On one occasion I saw
him pull a wounded Bosnian woman out of a ditch and get her to
safety while the Serbs were shooting at her. That took guts.
Though fortunately"—he chuckled reminiscently—"the Serbs
were mostly pretty awful shots. And they did get a bit nervous
about shooting at us, since unlike the unarmed civilians they usually shot at, we had a nasty habit of shooting back."

Twenty-Nine

The sky was bright, and overhead as always there were seagulls, wheeling and calling against the cliffs.

Officer James Harris of the United Kingdom Border Force glanced across the ferry terminal, lines of cars with hundreds of people, all waiting to board the cross-channel ferries. It was no longer the holiday season, but there was hardly ever a time when the Port of Dover wasn't busy.

His eye rested on a white Mercedes C300, Italian registered, at the UK Passport Control booth. An attractive, well-dressed couple were at that moment dealing with one of the assistant officers.

He frowned.

"Gordon," he said to the Assistant Officer beside him, "bring up that photofit picture they sent us from Exeter this morning will you? Those murder suspects."

Assistant Border Officer Gordon Lewis did so.

Harris peered at it, then back. "The pair dealing with Charlie Ferris," he said. "Take a quick glance. What do you think?"

Lewis glanced, and nodded. "Could be."

"All right, stay with me." Harris spoke softly into his Tetra radio. "Officer Ferris, ask the couple you're dealing with to pull off
to the side, will you? Then have them leave the car and accompa-
ny you to Interview Room 4. Be very casual. Tell them there's no
problem, just some routine paper work we need to fill out."

In the interview room he did his best to be geniality itself.

"Signor and Signora Sordi," he said, having looked at their
passports, which identified them respectively as Roberto Sordi
and Gina Sordi, "my apologies for all this. It's just a glitch over
some of your paperwork, and shouldn't take more than a few
minutes to put right. I understand you've been touring during the
last week. I hope that your visit to the United Kingdom has been a
pleasant one."

"Very pleasant, thank you."

"Most pleasant."

Their English was heavily accented. Which fitted the descriptions he'd been given.

"May I ask where you visited?"

"We went to Scotland for a while, and then to London, and
then also to your West Country."

"Good choices! And you were generally fortunate in your
weather, I believe—which is not, alas, always true of Scotland or
England." There was a knock at the door. "Excuse me. Yes!"

Gordon Lewis entered. He said nothing, but held out a sheet
of paper. Harris scanned it quickly.

"The Sordis' tyres," he read, "are Mercedes MOEs, and appear
to match the tyre prints found by Exeter CID near Soames' body.
Judging by what's in their luggage, their shoe sizes match the
footprints Exeter CID found by the body."

Harris nodded. "Thanks, Gordon. Stay here a moment, will
you?"

He looked back at his detainees.

"So — where did you visit in the west country?"

"Exeter."

"A beautiful city. I hope you were there mid-week. I always think it's the best time to visit. Everything gets so crowded at weekends."

Sordi looked at his wife.

"It was Tuesday," she said. "We stayed at an hotel called the White Hart."

"Ah yes! A good choice indeed: a delightful old inn. And did you spend all your time in the city? Or where you able to see some of the surrounding country?"

Sordi hesitated for a moment and then said, "We drove out to Haldon Belvedere. It is an interesting little folly."

"Delightful."

A skilled liar knows as a basic rule always to fashion a lie that's as close to the truth as possible. That way it's easier to re-member what you said, and your story is more likely — at least in part — to check out. If Sordi was lying he was following that rule. He'd accounted for their presence in Haldon village.

If, however, he *wasn't* lying, then a couple precisely matching the description of a pair of killers, even down to their accents and the size of their shoes, just *happened* to be in Haldon village on the day of the murder and just *happened* to have a car with the same tyres as the killers. Which was possible. People have been convict-ed of crimes they didn't commit as a result of coincidences no less bizarre. But still… it was a stretch.

Border Force officers in the United Kingdom had some powers of arrest, but they were limited to people who had committed, or were likely to have committed, offences under the Customs and Excise Acts. Suspicion of murder was rather different.

Harris scribbled on the note, "Fetch the police," and handed it back to Lewis, who was still waiting.

Lewis glanced at it, nodded non-committedly, and left.

Harris turned back to the couple.

"There will be just one more formality," he said. "My assistant is dealing with it, and then I think we can get you on your way in plenty of time for you to be where you ought to be."

THIRTY

Heavitree Police Station.
Monday, 3rd September

B right and early on Monday morning of the new week
Cecilia and Verity and Joseph were summoned to the Chief
Superintendent's office to find Glyn Davies himself there, though
he was still in not in uniform.

"I'll leave you people to it," the temporary replacement said.
"What I don't need to know I don't *want* to know."

As soon as he had left,

"There've been big developments in our case," Glyn Davies
said, "at least one of them completely unexpected. The unexpected one first! A sharp customs officer at Dover yesterday
morning spotted an Italian couple that looked like the photofit
pictures and descriptions you circulated of Soames' probable killers. He had them held for questioning and their car searched.
Long story made short—its tyre prints matched the tyre prints
Tom Foss and his cohorts found, and their feet sizes were right for
the footprints. Forensics in Dover then took the car in for examination, and last night they must really have got their finger out, because by this morning they had real results. In the glove

compartment they found an empty ampule, and it turns out it once held potassium chloride. What's more—and even more conclusive—they found traces of human hair and saliva in the boot, and the DNA matches Soames'."

He paused.

"So," he said, "as regards those who actually killed Soames and MacDonald and Patterson, I think we can say, 'Gotcha!'"

"Thanks to them having made some pretty big mistakes," Cecilia said.

"Huge mistakes! They should never have used their own car, or even stuck with the same car. In other words, as we thought from day one, as killers go they weren't the best. They killed efficiently, but they were careless."

"Luckily for us."

"Luckily for us. Ian Salmon is of course delighted, and *you*," he looked at Cecilia, "are definitely his Woman of the Year. He says, I'm to tell Detective Superintendent Cavaliere that 'her thoroughness paid off, and he was completely wrong to treat so lightly her decision to circulate the killers' description and the photofit pictures.' The fact is, Ian Salmon doesn't often admit to being wrong." He grinned. "Come to think of it, this is the first time I ever remember him actually *being* wrong—at least about anything that mattered!"

Cecilia did her best to look modest.

"Anyway," he continued, now including Verity in his address, "he wants you two to interview the couple and he's scheduled that for 11.00 a.m. tomorrow. He plans to observe. The question as to where they will eventually be tried is still moot, since several jurisdictions want a piece of them—the Met and the Scots as well as us. But until that's sorted out they're at Dover. I've arranged a car and driver for you tomorrow morning, but it's a four and half hour run, give or take, so it'll mean you leaving at 6:00 a.m. or a little before. I take it you're both up for that? It's an early start, but hopefully you should at least be home in reasonable time in the evening."

Cecilia and Verity nodded.

"Good," Davies said, "I'll confirm all that with Commander Salmon. Next item: moving on to developments that we *did* expect. Salmon is fairly sure that within the next twenty-four hours or so the NCA will have everything it needs to be able to complete its research on Mr Big—I think he told you both about all that?"

Cecilia and Verity nodded.

"Assuming that works out, on the day *following*—that's to say Wednesday—he wants to collect all four of us from here at ten in the morning. If everything goes as he hopes, we should be away from here for not more than four hours, and in that time finally be able to wrap up the murders you've been investigating. Joseph, if you can, he says he'd like you to bring with you something that will be able to detect electronic listening devices in a large room in a Georgian pile. Do you have anything portable that can do that?"

Joseph nodded slowly.

"An RF signal detector," he said. "And I think also a spectrum analyser, just in case we're up against something using multiple frequencies in rapid sequence—an RF detector wouldn't pick that up."

Glyn Davies smiled.

"Good," he said. "I take it that means 'yes'! Then I'll tell Ian that we're good to go on both appointments."

THIRTY-ONE

Dover Police Station in Ladywell
Tuesday morning, 4th September

For some reason that was doubtless known to some histori-
ans, in the short distance—less than a mile—between Maison
Dieu Road and the High Street in Dover, the B2245 found reason
to change its name no less than three times, starting off as Park
Street, then becoming Park Place, and finally debouching into the
High Street as Ladywell. Given this choice, Dover Police Station,
in itself a fairly nondescript red brick building, always insisted
that its address was Ladywell, despite the sign on the wall directly
opposite it that said, "Park Place." Was that because someone
thought "Ladywell" sounded better? Why would anyone think
that? Who knew?

Whatever the reasons for these whims and inconsistencies
(not to say follies and nonsense) Commander Salmon's driver
found the place without difficulty, and they arrived at 10.45 a.m.,
in good time for the commander to watch the scheduled interviews.

As he got out of the car his head and his arm were starting to
ache.

"Are you all right, sir?" said Nicholas Pickett, his driver. "You're looking a bit peaky. I've got some pain-killers in the glove compartment if they'd help."

The offer was tempting, but—

"Thank you, Nick," he said, "I'd better not. They tend to addle my brains, and if I'm to observe these interviews I think I'd best keep what few wits I have about me."

On entering the station he was glad to find Cecilia Cavaliere and Verity Jones already there, together with a Detective Superintendent Matthews from Dover police who would observe the interview. After brief preliminaries and such courtesies as are normal on such occasions, he had a word aside with Cecilia and Verity.

"I trust Glyn Davies told you I want you two to conduct these interviews," he said.

"Yes, sir."

"I watched you in Bristol. You work well together and under the circumstances your knowledge of Italian, Cavaliere, is an enormous bonus both for us and for the interviewees."

"I'll talk to them first in Italian," Cecilia said, "and make it clear they have a choice as to whether they're interviewed in English or Italian. If either of them choose the latter, it will be slower, but I'll simply translate my questions and their answers."

"Good," he said. "If I feel a need to ask a question of my own or intervene in some way, I'll let you know."

A short while later he and the Dover police officer seated themselves by the one-way window into the interview room.

At which point his mobile vibrated in his inside pocket. He took it out and turned away from the interview room window.

"Salmon here."

"Sir, I'm to tell you the Swiss have called back, and your suspicions were entirely correct. They're sending you the paper work and it should be here when you return this afternoon."

At last! He was beginning to be concerned that they wouldn't come through in time.

"Thank you," he said. "Please express my gratitude to our Swiss colleagues for their speedy co-operation."

"I will, sir."

He turned back to the scene in the interview room, where Roberto Sordi was already sitting with his solicitor. He looked tired, which was understandable, but otherwise well enough.

THIRTY-TWO

An interview room in Dover Police Station.
The same morning.

When Cecilia and Verity entered the interview room at a minute to eleven, the prisoner and his solicitor were already there. Cecilia began by addressing Sordi in Italian as she had said she would, explaining his options. He indicated his willingness to be interviewed in English.

"Very well," she continued in English. "If at any time you are not entirely sure what is being said, or that you are expressing yourself as you wish to, then use me as interpreter. I am, as I am sure you can see, perfectly bilingual."

Having next made sure that he was aware of his rights and responsibilities under English law, she proceeded to the actual interview, doing her best to speak clearly and precisely.

"Signor Sordi, you are aware, I trust, of the seriousness of the charges against you and Signora Sordi and the weight of the evidence?"

"I believe so."

"And you are aware that if found guilty you are liable to be sentenced to a very long term in prison?"

"I am."

"Let me make clear at once that nothing that transpires in this interview can affect those charges, or your standing trial on them, or the probable verdicts, or the sentences likely to be imposed. The Crown Prosecution Service of the United Kingdom will not allow anything approaching a plea bargain or *patteggiamento*, so whatever you have to tell me and however useful the authorities may find it, for better or worse there can be no question of any kind of deal over it."

Personally she was quite sure it was for better. She was aware that opinions on the question differed on both sides of the Atlantic, but in her view, any advantage judiciaries gained from plea bargaining in particular cases was far outweighed by the damage it did to the system overall. All too often what happened was that the cleverest crooks, who were also quite frequently the worst, bought themselves immunity by turning state's evidence at the right moment while the lesser fry went down.

"The most I can say," she said, "is that your co-operation with the police at this stage of our investigations will be likely to induce the court to view you more favourably, and that can hardly be to your disadvantage."

Sordi shrugged.

"I understand that. And given the situation, I intend to co-operate as far as I am able."

Evidently he was a realist. But his manner was listless, barely concerned. Which for some reason she found more disturbing than if he had been aggressive or defensive.

Still, she could do nothing about it, so she moved to the meat of her inquiry.

"Would you agree, Signor Sordi, that you and your wife are contract killers?"

"We are."

"And you were hired to come to this country to carry out a

number of specified hits on particular persons?"

"We were."

"How were you hired? Tell us what happened."

"My wife and I were staying at a hotel in Lugano on another job."

It would be interesting to know what the other job was. But she resisted the temptation to interrupt him.

"There was a message left for us with reception," he said. "It said, 'There is a job for you,' and there was a number to call. Nothing else."

"So?"

"So we called. Our call was answered by a man who asked us what would be our fee for killing three people in the United Kingdom over the next few weeks."

"Who was this man?"

Sordi shrugged. "I don't know. Our contact with him was entirely by phone. We always called that same number. Sometimes we'd call and there'd be no answer, but so far as I could tell when there was an answer it was always same voice. Sometimes, of course, he called us."

"What can you tell me about the voice?"

"As I've said, it was a man. And I think he perhaps went to a school for upper-class people, but... but...*ma non si è fatta una cultura.*"

"*Sì. Capito.* You are saying that although you think he went to good schools, he wasn't really a person of any culture?"

"That is right. I thought he was at heart... *come si dice?... volgare.*"

"Vulgar."

"*Sì.* Yes."

She nodded. The distinction he was making was quite subtle, and if he was right, then rather striking from someone with limited English. It also fitted rather well with Grimes' description of his boss as "posh".

"The number that you called—can you write it down for me?" she said.

"I can."

She pushed over a pad and pencil.

"Do so."

Sordi complied.

She looked at the result and shook her head. She didn't recognize it, and suspected it would be the number for yet another disposable phone.

"And you have no idea who this man is?" she said. "Or where he is?"

Again he shrugged. "None whatever."

She nodded. This was exactly the story Duncan Grimes had told. It was apparently Mr Big's way of keeping contact with his employees.

"So—you were asked how much you would charge to kill three people in the United Kingdom. What then?"

At this point Sordi's solicitor seemed willing to intervene, but Sordi shrugged and waved him aside.

"We agreed to do the three for €20,000," he said.

"Who were these people you were to kill?"

"An Andrew MacDonald, a Charles Soames, and a George Patterson."

She exchanged a look with Verity, who promptly took up the questioning.

"How would you find them?"

"We were provided with details of their appearance, places of residence, photographs, everything we needed."

"How was that done?"

"The materials were sent to us in a package, to an accommodation address in Italy."

"What kind of package?"

"Just a big yellow envelope, one of those with bubble wrap

inside. And it had a lot of English stamps on it."

"Do you remember the postmark?"

Sordi shook his head. "I suppose there was one, but I didn't notice what it was."

"Hmm. Who set up your accommodation address?"

"We did. We were told to set it up and then tell the man on the telephone what it was. He would then send us the materials. We would tell him when we had received them and were ready to go forward with the operation."

"And that's what happened?"

"That's what happened."

Thus the angel of death had gone quietly about his business.

"We shall want that address," Verity said.

The solicitor nodded. "I have it."

"Good. And how were you paid, Signor Sordi? How did you get your money?"

"The agreed sum was paid into a bank account in the Cayman Islands that we had opened earlier."

"And you received the whole lot? Twenty thousand euros? Just like that?"

"We were paid in instalments. As soon as we did each job we called and notified him and then the money was deposited — within minutes after we made contact, so far as we could see. It was very efficient. Six thousand for the first, six thousand for the second, and eight thousand for the last. As I said, twenty thousand in all."

Neat and tidy.

"We shall of course require details of that account and all those transactions."

"Of course." Sordi looked at his solicitor.

"I have those details too," the solicitor said. "I will let you have them."

When the interview was over, Cecilia found herself saddened

and disturbed. Roberto Sordi was a good-looking young man, evidently intelligent, even sensitive. And yet he had chosen this. And he didn't seem to care—either about what he had done, or even that he had been caught.

She sighed.

The truth was, she was glad to be out of his presence.

THIRTY-THREE

When Gina Sordi was brought into the interview room Cecilia found her disturbing for a different and rather more shocking reason. Gina Sordi reminded her of herself. She might have been looking at a sister. Only she hoped the expression in her eyes was not so full of scorn, so plainly contemptuous of everything and everyone around her.

Gina Sordi told essentially the same story as her husband — not, Cecilia noted, the same as with witnesses who have got together and agreed on what they are going to say. Her general experience was that whenever several people told her *exactly* the same story, the chances were she was listening to a rehearsed lie. In this case, she had the sense that overall she was hearing the truth, though from a different viewpoint.

Indeed very different! Where Roberto was dull and unconcerned, Gina was interested and even… the right English word for it escaped her for a moment and then came upon her with force… *gleeful* over what the two of them had done. As Gina talked it became ever more apparent that she had been the instigator, the inventor and the devising genius behind their work. Roberto was her listless accomplice… and in many ways, if the truth were told, her victim too. Indeed she claimed no less.

She was in some respects a rather better witness than her husband. She recalled details that he had not noticed or had forgotten — details, for example, about the package they had received with information that would enable them to identify their victims.

"The postmark was London," she said, "EC4. And one of the stamps had a picture of Big Ben on it."

"Why," Cecilia said to her at the end, "did you do this? You are young, healthy and intelligent. You could be doing anything you wanted. Why this?"

Gina Sordi shrugged.

"Life is so boring. At least killing people gets you to the edge. And think of the joke."

"The joke?"

"Well, here are all these people worrying about this and that and then you give them a little injection and pouf! It's all over, and none of it mattered anyway. And you have six thousand euros to spend! Isn't that a joke? And you're the joker! How cool is that! If life is a boring joke, best be the joker!"

"And you never wonder about the people you kill, who they are, who might care about them, or need them? Whose lives you might be ruining?"

"Do you like to eat chicken, *soprintendete* Cavaliere?"

"Sometimes, yes."

"So while you are enjoying your chicken — perhaps a delicious *costolette di pollo al Vermouth* — do you have anxiety attacks about the chicken's friends and relations?"

Cecilia exchanged a glance with Verity, who raised both eyebrows and gave a faint shrug.

It was surely time to bring this to a close.

"Do you have any further questions, Detective Inspector Jones?"

"No, ma'am."

Cecilia glanced at the clock and then got to her feet.

"Thank you, Signora Sordi," she said. "You have been most co-operative. Interview terminated at 12.26 p.m."

The truth was she would be even more relieved to be out of Gina Sordi's presence than she was that of her husband.

THIRTY-FOUR

Dover Police Station.
About half an hour later

I an Salmon stood thoughtfully in the cark park in the rear of Dover Police Station, where he had just taken leave of Cavaliere and Jones. It had been, overall, a profitable morning. As regarded the actual physical killings of Charles Soames, Andrew MacDonald and George Patterson, it was clear that they now had their culprits. That of course left the organizing mind behind it all, the real killer, still at large. Tomorrow they would do something about that.

Cecilia Cavaliere had said to him as they walked through the station after the interviews, "Gina Sordi reminded me in a way of me, sir. To tell you the truth, I found it a little unnerving."

He understood. The resemblance had struck him, too. And it had disturbed him very much, partly because — as he would admit to himself although certainly not to her or anyone else — he found Cecilia Cavaliere herself immensely attractive. And Gina Sordi really *was* like her. Not just superficially — both of them tall, slim, dark-haired and, of course, Italian. No, there was actually something about her profile, the tilt of her chin, and an occasional unthinking gesture with the hands that was precisely the same. An evil Cavaliere... if they'd been in a film the same actress could have played both parts... like the same actor playing Claudius and the Ghost in *Hamlet*.

He wondered if, some generations back, they were in truth biologically related.

It was conceivable.

They were, after all, both Italian.

A DNA test would tell.

He shook his head.

That was something he didn't need to know, and so far as he could see, neither did anyone else.

He sighed, and started to walk back to the front of the station where Nick had parked their car. Leaving aside his personal reactions to some of their interviewees, things overall were going well and he had every reason to feel satisfied. Nevertheless, his head was throbbing, his bruises ached, and the pain in his chest was giving him gyp. And of course, as he very well knew, it wasn't all a result of the explosion. Weeks before that, the doctors had been very clear about what was happening to him. They had told him he had months at most.

Click. Click. Click.

Even the tap of his walking stick on the paving stones was jarring. So what if Gina Sordi was right? What if life was all a bad joke? Had he not some reason to think that? Given the trick it had played on him? Given the time bomb in his body that would kill him?

Click. Click. Click.

And what of the world around him? More and more these days, and especially these last months, he found himself thinking of W. B. Yeats "Second Coming" — lines that had struck him even as a boy at Eton.

Things fall apart; the centre cannot hold;
Mere anarchy is loosed upon the world,
The blood-dimmed tide is loosed, and everywhere
The ceremony of innocence is drowned;
The best lack all conviction, while the worst
Are full of passionate intensity.

That had been true when Yeats wrote it in 1919 and he rather thought it was true now. Yeats had been fortunate enough to die in the warmth of France before the madness of World War II broke upon the world. Perhaps Ian Salmon should count himself lucky if he died while Great Britain was still a part of Europe, while, indeed the United Kingdom was still united, before the colossal mistake and betrayal that was "Brexit" had born its fruit. How ironic that those who voted for it triumphantly waved the Union flag, when it was entirely likely that what they had done would not only take Britain out of Europe but also end the four hundred year old union of England and Scotland, rendering obsolete the very flag they waved!

Which was no more than we deserved... Europe needed us and we chose to bail out... no wonder the French called us "perfide Albion"!

Click. Click. Click.

He stopped for a moment to get his breath.

So what would he do with whatever time he had left, months or weeks or even days? Of course he'd go on doing what he always did. Even if the ship were sinking or on a wrong course, he'd do what he could to help stuff the holes and bail it out and steer it as safely he could for as long as he could, since he could think of no other ship he'd rather be in nor anything else he'd rather do. And there were still a few things he might pull off in the time left to him, a few ways in which he hoped he could make some difference before the end, or at least (again he smiled and shook his head at his own vanity) before the end of *him*, which would certainly not be "the end".

Click. Click. Click.

At last he was back at the car.

And here was Nick his driver, rushing round to open the car door for him, concern in his eyes.

"Nick," he said as he sank gratefully into the back of the limousine, "if those pain-killers of yours are still on offer, I could really use them now."

THIRTY-FIVE

Exeter, Heavitree Police Station.
Tuesday, 4ᵗʰ October. 10.00 a.m.

As he had promised, Commander Ian Salmon arrived promptly at the Heavitree Police Station to collect them all at ten o'clock. Cecilia thought he looked drawn, but his manner was cheerful.

I could get used to this, she said to herself as she and the others settled into the back of the Jaguar XJ LWB limousine.

"Let me brief you," Salmon said as soon as they had pulled out of the Heavitree Police Station car park. "We're going to Colme Abbey in Somerset, which will be about an hour's drive, allowing for the morning traffic. Are you familiar with that?"

"It's the family seat of the Dukes of Caernwick, isn't it?" Joseph said. "Though I've never been there."

He pronounced Caernwick correctly.

"It is," Salmon said. "And we're going there now because that's where we will wrap up this business of the deaths of Bernard Standish and DI Sterling, as well as the murders and attempted murders of the 1986 black ops team. At the same time, I do *not* want the interview we have this morning leaked in any way, for reasons that I think will become apparent as we proceed. That's why when we arrive I'll want you, Joseph, to do a sweep of wherever we find ourselves working — which I rather imagine will be the duke's study in Colme Abbey — to make absolutely sure there's no surveillance."

Joseph nodded. "I can do that, sir."

"Good man. Cecilia, you have the phone number that Joseph lifted from McClintock's smartphone? — The number that Grimes used to call the person he took orders from?"

"I do, sir."

"And the number that Roberto Sordi gave you yesterday?"

"Yes, sir."

"Good. When we arrive at the Abbey, I'll be interviewing the duke. At some point during that interview, I'm going to ask you 'to make the calls that we talked about,' and I'll want you first to call the number that Joseph came upon, and then the number that Roberto Sordi gave you. I'm hoping our villain hasn't changed them yet."

"Got it, sir."

"I warn you all now, this is not going to be the kind of end to a murder investigation that one normally looks for, and in some respects will be unsatisfactory. The man we're going to talk to is responsible for all the murders you've been investigating as well as for the attempted murders. He didn't plant the bombs or give the lethal injections, but he paid others to do it and as far as I'm concerned that means he's the real killer. That's what I believe, and by the end of the morning I think you'll believe it too. Yet we won't be charging him with murder. Given various circumstances that will become evident as we proceed, I don't think that's possible. The charges we will bring will be less than murder. But they'll be serious charges involving serious prison time that we can prosecute successfully in the courts without endangering national security, and justice will more or less be served. I'm bringing you four in on it partly because your hard work has been an essential factor in our bringing this case to any conclusion at all and you deserve to be, so to speak, in at the kill, and partly because I want good investigating officers with me as I close out the enquiry, in case there's something I'm missing."

The others nodded. Cecilia found herself utterly intrigued and fascinated by these developments.

"Is the duke expecting us?" she asked. "I take it he's your suspect?"

"He is indeed," Salmon said. "And he's certainly expecting someone from the Nation Crime Agency." He glanced at Glyn Davies and gave a wry smile. "But no, I don't think he's actually expecting *us!*"

THIRTY-SIX

The law offices of Garland, Garland, and Garland
Ropemaker Street, London EC2Y.
10:55 a.m. the same day

The clock on the wall in front of Henry Garland's desk—the clock that so far as he knew had been ticking away there since 1874, save for occasional breaks for cleaning and once for repair and replacement of parts—that same clock had just given the odd little creak that it always gave at five minutes to the hour, as it worked itself up (so it seemed to him) to chime, when he was stirred from his morning of quiet legal industry by the sound of sirens from beyond the office windows. Ambulances? Police cars? The Fire Brigade? If there was a way of distinguishing between them, he didn't know what it was. But without doubt he was hearing emergency vehicles of some kind, and there were surely several of them.

Unable to resist his curiosity, he pushed aside the Last Will and Testament of Joachim Obadiah Hicks, which was at that moment occupying his attention, or at least supposed to be occupying it, got to his feet, walked over to the window and peered down. The scene in the street below went some way toward rewarding whatever hopes he may have had for high drama and something to tell Philippa when he got home that evening. On the opposite side of the road two police cars, their sirens now silent but their lights still flashing, were parked outside the premises of Dillon and Quincy. As he watched, there were more sirens and lights from the direction of Moorgate: a third police car arrived, followed by a police van. Uniformed officers from both vehicles moved into the building. Inevitably a crowd of the idle curious and those with nothing better to do was beginning to form.

How did he know they were idle and had nothing better to do? He shook his head, struck by his own willingness to categorize pejoratively an entire group of whom he actually knew nothing.

Did not he himself have several better things to do that he was not doing—such as perusing the Last Will and Testament of Joachim Obadiah Hicks? And yet here he was, indulging his curiosity with the best of them, only privileged in that he could do so privately from the second floor window of Garland, Garland, and Garland, thereby shielded in his weakness from the common gaze?

And now, real excitement! He bent forward to get a better view. The police were bringing men out of the building. Two—no, three of them. Respectable looking men in suits and ties: respectable looking, that is, except for the fact that they were handcuffed and shame-faced and evidently in police custody.

They were inserted into the two first police cars, which drove rapidly away, sirens again wailing and lights flashing. After a moment or so, more police officers emerged through the big front doors. These were carrying files and boxes and computers, which they started to load into the van.

The door to Henry Garland's office opened with a soft click, and he turned as Bob Palmer his secretary entered, bearing files and papers of their own.

"Any idea what's going on, Bob?" he asked, reasonably certain that his secretary would know exactly what was going on.

"Word on the street sir is some of the folks at Dillon and Quincy's went fishing in the wrong pond and got caught red-handed with their fingers in the till."

Henry Garland nodded, following this mixture of metaphor with an ease that came from well over thirty years of familiarity with its source.

"They tell me," Bob Palmer continued, "it's something to do with all those millions of American money for Iraq that went missing a while back, after the war. Someone seems to have decided they could give it a good home here."

It sounds as if they thought it was a puppy, Garland reflected. But he said nothing. This was too good to interrupt.

"Anyway, sir, believe it or not, the law's gone and nicked the Earl of Arden for it and a couple of other Dillon and Quincy blokes who were in on it with him. Just brought them out. That's what I heard, anyway. From my sources," he concluded loftily.

Henry nodded. His experience over thirty years was that Bob Palmer's "sources" were right most of the time. Quite who they were or how they invariably came by so much accurate information within seconds of an event was, like many things in this life, a mystery to him. But it was a mystery with which he was content to live.

And he would certainly have something of interest to tell Philippa when he got home tonight.

THIRTY-SEVEN

Colme Abbey in Somerset
The same morning.

"Impressive!" Cecilia said, as they swept up a wide drive toward the imposing Georgian façade.

"Ah, yes. But would you want to live here?" Ian Salmon asked her.

She laughed.

"No," she said, "I wouldn't! Too much flat grass, for one thing!"

He smiled and nodded his agreement.

"Neither would I," he said. "Still, I grant you it's impressive. Interestingly enough, there was once a fine avenue of elm trees leading up to the house. I've seen pictures of them in old prints. But they were taken down in 1803 as part of 'improvements' by the then duke."

Just like the idiot Rushton in *Mansfield Park*, Cecilia reflected.

Though Salmon had agreed that the house was impressive, he didn't seem especially impressed when they entered.

"Thank you," he said to the man who opened the front door. "I'm from the National Crime Agency. I believe we're expected. I know the way."

At once, as one familiar with the place, he led them up a wide formal staircase to a door on the second floor, where he rapped with his walking stick and entered without waiting for an answer.

"Good morning, your grace," he said to an elderly man behind a large desk at the far end of a handsome, book-lined room.

The man rose to his feet, his face registering shock and consternation.

"*Salmon!*" he said. And then, "*Davies!* Good God, I thought you two were both..."

He stopped.

To Cecilia's utter surprise, Ian Salmon suddenly spread out his arms, walking stick and all, and then, waving them about, glided towards the duke's desk like a schoolboy pretending to be a ghost.

"Oooo! Ooooo!" he moaned, and then, "*Dead?* Is that what you were going to say? You thought we were both dead?"

"I... no... well, everyone thought... there was a rumour... I mean, of course, I'm delighted to see you both alive and well."

Salmon nodded. "Of course you are! Thoroughly delighted! Allow me to present the rest of our team, Detective Superintendent Cecilia Cavaliere, Detective Inspector Verity Jones, and Mr Joseph Stirrup, all of them from Exeter CID. We have several things we need to discuss with you."

"I was told the NCA wanted to talk about financial matters."

"In a sense that's true. But you may have been somewhat misled as to precisely what kind of financial matters — or indeed into thinking that finance was the only thing we're going to discuss. And I'm afraid I'm to blame for that. What with that and our not being dead, I'm afraid Glyn Davies and I are being rather a nuisance this morning. That said, I'm extremely anxious that what we *are* here to discuss shall remain in this room. Mr Stirrup, may I call on your expertise? Are we clear of listening devices?"

"It'll take me a few minutes to be sure, sir," Joseph said, unzipping the bag he was carrying and beginning to produce his gadgets.

At which the duke recovered enough to protest.

"Bugger it, Salmon, what the hell is this?"

"It's me taking precautions in the name of national security," the commander replied calmly. "Although when I come to think about it, it might be argued they're just as much in your interest as they are in the interests of the United Kingdom. Take your time, Mr Stirrup. We are in no hurry."

Joseph began his work.

"As for the rest of us," Commander Salmon said, "I dare say it will be calming for us if we sit down. Including you," he added, gesturing toward the duke.

In distinctly strained silence the group seated itself and waited while Joseph performed his rituals, limping a little today, but surely not nearly as badly as he had been a couple of weeks back. Cecilia glanced at Verity, who merely gave a faint smile, as to say, "Don't worry. He's enjoying himself!"

Finally Joseph said, "There's no sign of any listening device, sir."

"Thank you Mr Stirrup. And now, your grace,"—he turned back to the duke—"there are a lot of questions to be answered."

"If you think," the duke said, "that I'm going to answer questions after your barging in here like this, you've got another think coming. I'd send for the police, except... except..."

He hesitated.

"I know," Salmon said, "except that we *are* the police. Awkward, isn't it? Well, never mind! If you won't talk, I will. I'm going to tell you a story. And it's all about you."

THIRTY-EIGHT

Colme Abbey, the duke's study
A few minutes later

Cecilia watched fascinated as Commander Salmon paused, limped to the window, and looked out, perhaps gathering his thoughts. As the daylight fell on his face, she was again struck by how drawn he looked, how tired.

Yet when he turned back and faced the duke and spoke, his voice was firm and strong.

"In 1986," he said, "you were in charge of Section F of the Intelligence Service—a position of considerable power and influence. You abused that position, first, by authorizing secret involvement by British intelligence in the Iran-Contra transfers, against the expressed wishes of both the government of the United Kingdom and the congress of its ally the United States of America, and by involving the firm of Dillon and Quincy in those transactions. Secondly, you diverted considerable sums of money from that enterprise to your own personal use. To be precise, you arranged for them to be syphoned by Dillon and Quincy to a criminal called Duncan Grimes, who in turn used his contacts to turn them over to a financial services company in the Cayman Islands called Impresa Gabriella, specialists in money laundering, who rendered them pure and clean for transfer to a Swiss bank account in your and your son's names—an account, of course, to which in 1986 Her Majesty's Revenue and Customs would not have had access."

"Outrageous," the duke said. "I'd like to see you try to prove any of that."

Which in Cecilia's experience was what people always said when they knew they were guilty but thought you couldn't make it stick. Ian Salmon continued, however, as though the duke had not spoken.

"It then came to your ears that one Bernard Standish, a prominent investigative journalist, was working on a story about all this and was coming very near to uncovering and publishing the truth. You—again abusing your position of power in the security services—organized a black bag operation utilizing officer cadets from Sandhurst to ascertain whether this was really so. When as a result of that operation it became clear to you that Bernard Standish was indeed onto you and about to reveal your dealings, you used contacts you had at the Russian embassy to have him run down in the street."

The duke spluttered angrily, but Commander Salmon merely raised an admonitory finger.

"I haven't finished yet! There's more of this cloak and dagger tale to come! So then... one DI Sterling, a shrewd and capable Metropolitan police officer, was assigned to investigate. He was puzzled by two aspects of the affair. The former was, what kind of large black car could have been seen by so many people and yet identified by none of them? He correctly guessed that it was a Russian Zil limousine. The latter was the identity of the man who pulled Bernard Standish's son back from being run down with his father, and then disappeared. I imagine that man was someone you sent to make sure the job was done—and my best guess is, your son, who was then working in a fairly junior capacity for the security services. I think it quite possible he was meant to push the boy as well as his father into the car's path, but then found himself too much observed to be able to get away with it, or maybe lost his nerve, or maybe even had a moment of decency and simply couldn't do it—anyway, he pulled him back instead, and then disappeared from the scene as quickly as possible.

"When DI Sterling seemed to be getting dangerously near to the truth of all this and had informed his superiors of his suspicions, you again abused your position of power by getting the entire story suppressed and the evidence destroyed for what were alleged to be reasons of national security."

He paused.

"Right! So how does this sound to you so far?" he said. "I am open to criticism and critique."

"An impertinent bloody fantasy," the duke said.

"That's all you have to say? Well then, let me continue. Earlier this year, some thirty years after the events I've just described, you learn to your horror that the enquiry into Bernard Standish's death is actually to be re-opened. I confess, at first I couldn't for the life of me see just *how* you learnt this. It wasn't exactly headline news! So my little story had a serious gap in it. But then one of my staff, whom I've had researching your life and career for several days, discovered, lo, that you were at Paddington Green Police Station, the very station which was to re-open the enquiry into Standish's death, on September the 14th of this very year, mere days after they'd been asked to do it! You were there to open the newly furbished wing... a touching moment, incidentally: a noble duke giving his gracious blessing to the humdrum labours of ordinary coppers. Let me admit that even now, just *exactly* how you found out about the soon-to-be-re-opened enquiry is a mystery to me. Did some zealous officer think to show you how carefully the Metropolitan police check even old cases? Was it part of a series of examples offered for your admiration? Or did you merely stumble on it by luck—perhaps you noticed a file on someone's desk? I have no idea."

Cecilia realized that she was holding her breath, so taken was she by this narrative and the duke's reaction to it.

"I *do* know, however," Salmon continued, "that you were at Paddington Green Police Station on the 14th and that all hell broke loose a few days' later. And supposing *that* to have been mere coincidence is a bit of a stretch. Less of a stretch is this: having discovered *somehow* that the case that involved you was to be reopened, you decided on the Carl von Clausewitz approach—total war. There was too much at stake for you to be satisfied with half measures. So you would take out *everyone* who might have seen Standish's material, which meant the five men who were originally involved in the black ops break-in at Standish's home, and the police officer who investigated his death. You recruited two sets of contract killers to carry out those killings—one set, it transpires, proving rather more efficient than the other, though even they were careless in some respects—but then, in my experience contract killers are like plumbers and electricians: people who need their services are always trying to find a good one."

The duke seemed about to interrupt, but Commander Salmon held up his hand.

"I gave you a chance to criticize and critique earlier, and you didn't take it. I'm in full flow now, so you'll have to wait. So then... covering up your old crimes wasn't your only concern in this year of grace 2016. By no means! You are an energetic old fellow! Through your contacts in the intelligence services and the world of international crime you'd recently found a way to gain access to some of those billions of dollars of American money that we all know went missing from Iraqi reconstruction. And you decided that what worked a few decades earlier would surely work again. Dillon and Quincy could get the money to Duncan Grimes

and his cohorts, Grimes and company could get it to Impresa Gabriella—hence those moving scenes played out at the Royal Portsbury Dock—and Impresa Gabriella could launder it for your
Swiss account. This time, however, the scheme seems to have
gone wrong. The authorities have taken possession of the stolen
money, Grimes and his associates are in custody, and they're all
spilling lots of beans!"

He paused, and looked at his watch.

"Detective Superintendent Cavaliere," he said, "I believe it
may now be time to add a new medium to this morning's presen-
tation. Please make the first of those phone calls we spoke of earlier."

"Yes, sir," Cecilia said, by no means displeased to have a role
in the unfolding drama. She took her phone out of her handbag,
and stabbed in a number.

Less than a second later there was a ring from the duke's desk.

"Hadn't you better answer that?" Salmon said. "You can do it
conveniently while Detective Superintendent Cavaliere is making
her call."

"There's no need. I can call back later."

"I insist you answer it, your grace. If not, I'm going to ask
Chief Superintendent Davies to answer it for you. And should you
be keeping that phone in a locked drawer, I authorize him now to
force it open if he has to."

As he said this he took from his pocket and pulled on a pair of
white cotton gloves.

The duke muttered something scatological, opened the drawer
to his right, and pulled out a mobile phone.

"Yes," he said into it, the single syllable echoing from the
phone in Cecilia's hand even before he had completed it.

"Thank you, Detective Superintendent." Salmon moved to the
desk and gently but firmly removed the phone from the duke's
hand, carefully holding it by its edges. "I think, your grace, that

we may need this in evidence. Would you take charge of it for us, Detective Inspector Jones?"

"Yes, sir."

Verity produced an evidence bag from her handbag, and Commander Salmon dropped the phone into it.

"And now, if you will, the second call, Detective Superintendent Cavaliere?"

Cecilia stabbed in the second call, again a phone rang in the duke's desk, and again Ian Salmon took it and passed it to Verity.

"Thus," he said, "with the first telephone we establish your connection with Duncan Grimes and his group, and the entire plan to launder the Iraq money, all of which was being carried out under your direction. With the second we establish your connection with Gina and Roberto Sordi, the murderers of Andrew MacDonald, Charles Soames, and George Patterson. The Sordis were, of course, also acting under your instructions."

Commander Salmon paused for a moment, but only for breath. He was by no means finished.

"Finally," he said, "there are further financial matters to be considered. I mentioned earlier that in the process of your unauthorized and illegal involvement of British intelligence resources in the Iran-Contra affair, you diverted considerable sums of money from that enterprise to your own personal use, and that these were placed in a Swiss bank account to which, in 1986, Her Majesty's Revenue and Customs would not have had access.

"Thanks, however, to our recent agreement with the Swiss authorities we are now able to examine such accounts in detail where we have reason to suspect tax evasion—of which indeed you and your son are both guilty, though that is the least of your crimes. We can now confirm massive sums placed to that account in 1986 by Impresa Gabriella, and, most interestingly, *further* massive sums in December 1990. These latter appear to have been funds intended for the first Gulf War, diverted to your own use through the same channels as before—"

His mobile phone rang.

"One moment."

He answered, listened for several moments, and nodded.

"Good. Thank you."

He turned back to the duke.

"The other little patch in our quilt," he said, "is now sewn into place. That was a colleague from the City of London Police. He tells me that at eleven o'clock this morning they arrested your son the Earl of Arden and two accomplices of his from Dillon and Quincy on charges of tax evasion, fraud, and money laundering. They're at present in custody at Wood Street Police Station, and are to appear in court tomorrow. So what do you think of my little fantasy now?"

THIRTY-NINE

Colme Abbey, the duke's study.
A few minutes later.

The duke—with, Cecilia thought, something of an effort—recovered himself. He gave a faint smile, spent a moment rearranging the papers on his desk, and then sat back in his chair.

"I think, Commander Salmon," he said finally, "that your fantasy is just what I said it is—a fantasy, and not even a very good one. Legally, of course, as a case against me or anyone else, we both know that it is worthless. To begin with, I took absolutely no action in any of the matters which you mention for which I did not have authority."

"Certainly you had authority," Salmon said. "The question at issue is your abuse of that authority for personal gain."

"Which cannot be demonstrated!" the duke retorted. "A great deal of what you allege couldn't possibly be presented in court, since to argue it you'd need to reveal details of British intelligence and security. You'd have to declassify what can't be declassified. Aside from that your evidence for virtually everything else you allege is circumstantial, and doubtless much even of that was obtained illegally. How, for example, did you acquire the first of those telephone numbers that you just used so theatrically? Did you have authorization for a tap? I'm sure you didn't! Intelligence service methods are all very well when you're working for the intelligence services, but hardly when you propose to bring someone to court! You say the police in London have arrested my son. Actually, you don't haven't anything on either of us, and as soon as you arrest *me*, which you must do if you are serious, we'll soon see which of us is better at playing this game."

During the early part of this speech Ian Salmon had begun to look at his notes, as if he found the speaker of no further interest. But then at the word "game" his mouth tightened, he turned back to the duke, raised his stick and brought it down on the duke's desk with a crash that scattered the just-rearranged papers and seemed to shake the room.

Cecilia felt the hairs rise on the back of her neck, and the duke visibly cowered.

"This *game?*" the commander said, glaring down at him. "Is that what this is for you, sir? A *game?* You find it *amusing?* Then let me be clear. It does not amuse *me*. Because of your greed and treachery decent people are dead—a fine journalist, a fine police officer, a beloved schoolteacher who'd also served his country under fire, and others—all of them people whose boots you weren't fit to lick. And now you think to benefit *from due process of law?*"

"I don't—"

"Listen to me carefully, your grace. Even if my colleagues and I don't have a case to bring to court, we now *know* that you are guilty—as, incidentally, do you. So what follows? I'll tell you what follows. First, as tends to happen in jobs where you're caught cheating on both your employers and the customers, you're fired."

He glanced again at his watch.

"What that means in practical terms as far as you are concerned is that from about an hour ago, all the contacts that you and your son had in the intelligence community, in law enforcement, and in finance, are dead. We've put out on both of you what our American friends call 'a burn notice' — a colourful expression that nicely makes the point. Your bridges are burnt! Any bank accounts you had access to, any credit cards — they're all frozen. You have nothing."

"I—"

"But that's the easy part, which I grant you is not easy. Then there is the hard part. There are powerful people in government and the intelligence services who are angry with you, very angry indeed... powerful people who aren't as squeamish as I am about capital punishment... powerful people who'll look at the deaths and mayhem you've caused, at your abuse of trust and authority and your manipulation of power, and demand eye for eye and tooth for tooth. If those people decide that your life and your son's life are to be nasty, brutish and short, then nasty, brutish and short they will be. And I think it by no means unlikely that they will decide exactly that. And why should they not? What are you, after all, but a well-born psychopath? A foul-mouthed killer who is a disgrace to his rank?"

He stopped. There was a moment of stunned silence.

The duke had gone white. At last, it seemed, Salmon had got to him.

"Then what should I do?" he said at last, and now his voice was weak. "How can I stop it?"

"My God!" Salmon said scornfully. "Even now the assumption of entitlement! The presumption of privilege! You *can't* stop it. I told you. It's already happening."

"But my boy... he's always done what I told him... What can I do to save him? It doesn't matter about me."

Salmon pursed his lips and stared at him judicially.

"A moment almost of unselfishness!" he said. "Amazing! And

why on earth should I or anyone else give a tuppenny damn about what happens to either of you?"

"Please!"

The commander considered a moment longer.

"I see one possibility for you," he said finally, glancing again at his watch. "In a few moments the police—that is, Somerset police—should be arriving with warrants for your arrest, which in the first instance will be on charges connected with what happened at the Royal Portbury Dock on Sunday night. Your only hope, as I see it, is not to argue with these charges, now or at any point. Admit to everything: the misuse of funds in 1986 and 1990, the billion-dollar theft of Iraqi money now, the money laundering, and the tax evasion over decades—everything that doesn't involve issues of national security. These are in themselves serious crimes to which you'll both plead guilty, and of course if found guilty of them you'll both go to prison for a very long time. But that'll be a payment that may just satisfy your creditors. And it may save your son's life. It's probably the best you can do. At any rate it's the best I can offer."

It was, Cecilia reflected, hardly an entirely satisfactory result from anyone's point of view—which was, indeed, exactly what Commander Salmon had warned them to expect. But justice would be served after a fashion. And given the circumstances and the national security issues involved it was, as he had also said, probably about the best that could be managed. She smiled inwardly. There was a time when she would have lost sleep over that "best that could be managed", but time had taught her—she hoped for the better—to be a little more patient than she once was with the imperfections of human justice and its administration.

Commander Salmon turned away from the duke and walked to the window.

"Ah," he said looking down, "and here are our friends from

the Somerset and Avon Constabulary, pat upon their cue."

He looked back again at the duke.

"Oh, and by the way," he said, "I forgot to mention. They're bringing with them a warrant to search these premises. I find it hard to imagine they'll find nothing of interest. And given that warrant of course anything they do find will certainly be admissible in court as evidence against you. All shipshape and above board, you know. Just as it should be!"

FORTY

O nce the duke had been formally arrested, he seemed to recover an element of bravado.

"Whatever you may say, Salmon, dog eats dog and that's all there is to it. It's the law of the jungle, and it's the only law that lasts. Today you happen to be the biggest dog. That's all. Nothing for you to look so bloody self-righteous about."

Ian Salmon, who was consulting with the senior Somerset and Avon police officer, looked up at the duke for a moment, shook his head, and went back to his conversation.

Obviously, Cecilia thought, the duke's father didn't read *The Jungle Book* to him when he was small, or he'd have known that "dog eats dog" isn't the law of the jungle at all. Papa used to read *The Jungle Book* to her in Italian when she was little, and she could still remember parts of it better in that language than in English. But there was one part she always remembered in Kipling's own words, which she'd learnt later and loved:

*Now this is the Law of the Jungle – as old and as true as
    the sky,*
*And the Wolf that shall keep it may prosper, but the Wolf
    that shall break it must die.*
*As the creeper that girdles the tree trunk, the law runneth over
    and back;*
*For the strength of the pack is the wolf, and the strength of the
    wolf is the pack.*

Following the duke's arrest, there were a few minutes delay in the arrangement of transport to their various destinations, and as they were standing in front of the house waiting for things to be sorted out, Cecilia found herself for a moment next to him. On impulse she turned to him.

"When a wolf pack is on the move," she said, "the most vulnerable wolves—the elderly, the pregnant females, and the very young—are always put at the centre of the pack. That's so that the strong wolves—the fighting wolves—can defend them."

He stared at her.

"Why are you telling me this?" he said.

"Because *that's* the law of the jungle. I just thought you ought to know."

When the handcuffed duke had finally been led away by Somerset and Avon police, and their own group returned to Commander Salmon's car, Cecilia was surprised, glancing at her watch, to see that they had actually been in Colme Abbey for a little over an hour and a quarter. It had, however, been a bruising hour and a quarter and it felt more like half a day.

Everyone, she sensed, was relieved that the business was over. They pulled away from the looming Georgian pile in a not uncomfortable silence, which was finally broken by Verity.

"May I ask you a question, sir?" she said to the commander.

"Certainly you may," he said. "And who knows? I may even try to answer it!"

"I can see," she said, "how once you were onto the duke and had people researching him, the story came together—the Swiss bank accounts, his being at Paddington Green Police Station on the 14th and so on. What I don't understand is what made you decide to look at him in the first place. I mean, if I've thought about him at all, I've always thought of him as a bit of an old bore—but a pillar of rectitude!"

Ian Salmon chuckled. "A pillar of rectitude! His public persona! Yes, he's been rather good at that, hasn't he?"

He paused.

"Spotting him was basically a matter of applying what I know about our intelligence agencies and the resources I have at the National Crime Bureau to the information that you people gathered. Which, in case I'm not making myself clear, is one way of saying I couldn't have done it without all of you.

"Following from Detective Superintendent Sterling's shrewd and thoughtful investigation, and what you and Superintendent Cavaliere learned of it, and then your team's analysis, you may recall I said that I would cogitate and consult. I did. My starting point was that you were obviously right—given the time span, we had to be looking for someone who was involved and powerful in the security services in 1986 and *still* able to be active, indeed murderous, thirty years later. Given human mortality, that narrowed the field of possible suspects a lot. In fact when I presented those parameters to my researchers, they were able to give me a list that began to look almost manageable... reduced, as I recall, to nine persons."

Cecilia was glad he'd mentioned Greg Sterling. It was some small satisfaction that his work should be seen for what it was—a first step along the road that led to the eventual nailing of his killers.

"Could I narrow the field even further?" Salmon said. "It occurred to me it was unlikely anybody British would have been involved in the Iran-Contra business unless it was for profit. Follow the money, as Deep Throat said! So what about looking at our candidates' bank accounts? Large and unaccounted-for deposits in 1986 would surely be an indicator of something? So I had our people check banking records for the nine (sounds a little like *The Lord of the Rings*, doesn't it?) and lo—there was nothing reprehensible! All were squeaky clean. What then, I asked myself, about overseas accounts? Did any of my candidates for villainy have such accounts? I started with what seemed the obvious places—the Cayman Islands and Switzerland. The Caymans were easy. Of course they're still a British Overseas Territory and a request from London carries some weight. Anyway, there wasn't anything there, or at least there was nothing that we could see. Then there were the Swiss. *That* was what took most of the week. The Bank of Switzerland isn't exactly ungracious or uncooperative, especially when it's been presented with evidence of malfeasance, but it is, let us say, somewhat ponderous in its proceeding."

Cecilia hid a smile. Ian Salmon might have been describing himself, although to tell the truth she was coming to enjoy him.

"Anyway," he continued, "it turned out that two of my potential suspects *did* have Swiss bank accounts. One of them, well, his wife is Swiss and they have family there, which seemed explanation enough. There were certainly no extraordinary sums in it, and nothing to attract my interest. To be honest, I'm not entirely sure about the legality of that account in 1986, but like good Queen Bess, I'd no desire to make windows into men's souls and I had (to mix my metaphors horribly) other fish to fry. But the other account! That belonged to the Duke of Caernwick, and that was another matter entirely. As you heard me point out to him this morning—he had a *massive* influx of funds in 1986, as well as another in 1990.

"I was now virtually certain we had our man. After that it was as you said, Verity, just a matter of having him researched and watching the pieces come together. The Swiss agreed to send us documented confirmation of the duke's transactions that could be used in evidence, and those arrived yesterday afternoon. At last I had, as our American friends say, my ducks in a row!"

He really rather enjoys his Americanisms, Cecilia thought. She found it quite endearing in someone so quintessentially English.

"Meanwhile," Salmon continued, "Grimes and company, having being caught red-handed with the Iraqi money—thanks of course to all of you!—have spilled lots of beans about how it got here, including the serious involvement of the duke's son as well as at least two more of the staff from Dillon and Quincy. Hence their arrest in London this morning!

"I also noticed several payments *out* of the duke's Swiss account during the last couple of weeks, payments to a Caymans Islands account in the name of Roberto and Gina Sordi. I guessed what those were for. When they themselves told you yesterday that those sums were precisely what they received, well, that was just one more confirmation.

"You'll be interested to know that the duke's Swiss account shows similar sums paid to a *second* Cayman Islands account, this one in the names of Yuri Ivanov and Ivan Andropov. That sounds like Russians, so we checked with the Russians though Interpol and lo, they've been surprisingly co-operative. There! Listen to me! I'm still enough of an old cold-war warrior to be surprised when the Russians co-operate. Anyway, the Russians tell us that they do indeed know about a pair of violent criminals called Yuri Ivanov and Ivan Andropov. They're both ex-Spetsnaz—that's

Russian Special Forces. They're trained in just the kind of improvised bomb-making our second pair of killers used and they're renegades. The Russians were already after them for blowing up an armored truck and robbing a bank in Moscow, but didn't even realize that they'd left Russia. Thanks to their being ex-Spetsnaz, we now have all the information about them we could want: photographs, fingerprints, even DNA. I don't think we'll get them in the UK this time round, but their descriptions are out worldwide, everyone is after them, and someone, I dare say, will get them in the end."

He paused.

"So you see," he said, "it was all quite easy, really."

Cecilia smiled to herself.

Lots of things are easy… once you know how they are done.

FORTY-ONE

Exeter. Saint Mary's Rectory.
The same day, late afternoon.

That afternoon, when Cecilia returned home, there was a white Ford Fiesta parked in front of the rectory gate.

She turned into the drive just in time to see the big front door open and Brenda Cosgrove and Bob Coulter emerge onto the porch with Michael, with whom they were laughing.

Brenda blushed prettily when she saw Cecilia, which amused Cecilia very much. She did not normally think of PC Brenda as at all the blushing type. But then—

"Hello, ma'am," Brenda said. "We're going to have pre-marital counselling with Father Michael."

"Why, that's lovely Brenda. Well done, Bob! I congratulate you both!"

Bob Coulter grinned.

"To tell you the truth, ma'am, I can't think what she sees in me. I must be a lucky bloke!"

"I think you are both lucky," she said.

"As I remember," she said to Michael when they were in the rectory later, "you told me you thought they were getting hot and heavy. Obviously you were right."

"Yes I was, to some extent. But I gather it was Bob's going undercover for this murder investigation that really got things heated up. Brenda missed him and worried about him and generally got herself into a state. And then—well, it was her birthday last week and while he was in London he sent her a bunch of crimson roses. And she didn't even realize he *knew* it was her birthday!"

Cecilia laughed. "Il rosso è il colore dell'amore! "

"So red's the colour of love, is it? Is that an Italian proverb?"

She smiled. "It's from a song I used to hear on the radio when I was little."

"Well anyway, apparently that did it. Our Brenda completely lost it! As soon as Bob re-appeared—I mean according to them *literally* the minute he drove into the car park—she spotted him from a window, rushed out to him before he'd even got out of his car, got in beside him, and asked him to marry her!"

"Did she now? How wonderfully modern of her!"

"Modern? *I* thought it was rather romantic."

"Can one actually *be* romantic in Heavitree Police Station car park?"

"Absolutely. In fact, it's just the kind of place that needs it."

"All right. So what happened next? Presumably he said 'yes'."

"'With alacrity!' he says. Those are his exact words. He says he'd never have had the nerve to propose to her himself, so once she'd asked him he certainly wasn't going to risk giving her a chance to change her mind!"

Cecilia shook her head. She found it hard to imagine Sergeant Bob Coulter, who disarmed thugs who had guns as if it were a walk in the park, being nervous about anything.

"I didn't even know they were C of E," she said.

"They're not—or at least not yet. She was baptized and confirmed RC but says she hasn't been since she was a little girl, so it's hardly poaching. Bob's not even baptized. But he's interested in the faith. So we're going to have some instruction together as a prelude to the pre-marital counselling, and see where that gets us."

"They're very different from each other."

"I dare say they are. And that's what lots of people say about you and me!"

She laughed. "That's true." She paused. "It's nice they came to you."

"I have you to thank for that. Apparently they were wondering who they could go to and talk about getting married, and then Brenda said, 'Cecilia Cavaliere puts up with Father Michael, so I dare say he's all right,' and Bob agreed, and so here they are."

"Well," she said, "I had no idea I was such a gift to the mission of the church."

There was a sound of paws clattering on parquet, and then a six-year-old voice came from the top of the stairs.

"Ciao, mama!"

She looked up to the child safety gates at the top of the stairs to see wide eyes and a waving tail beyond them.

"Ciao, tesoro! Ciao Figaro!"

And now behind them she could see mama leading little Rosina by the hand.

"Ciao, mama! Ciao, Rosina!"

She looked back at Michael and raised an eyebrow.

Evidently it was time to start thinking about supper.

"I'll put some water on while you take your coat off and say hello to everyone," he said. "Papa's going to join us as soon as he's finished at the university. Fettucine alla papalina stasera, sì?"

"Sì, amore."

FORTY-TWO

London.
The Central Criminal Court, Old Bailey, EC4.
Some weeks later.

For various reasons that no doubt seemed good to those who decide such things, it was determined that the trial of George St John Aloysius Eliot, Duke of Caernwick, and his son George Frederick Aloysius Eliot, Earl of Arden, on charges of theft, money laundering, fraud and tax evasion would take place not at the Crown Court in Bristol, as Cecilia at first expected, but in London at the Old Bailey in December. She would be required to attend and would be called as a witness.

The police search of Colme Abbey had indeed produced further evidence of the criminal activities of the duke and his son — evidence that implicated not only them, but contacts and associates in the United States and Iraq — evidence that had been passed to the authorities in both countries. The FBI had moved promptly and already made several arrests.

Cecilia could not help noticing the irony of it all. If the duke had not by mere chance seen the Bernard Standish file in Paddington Green Police Station, panicked over it, and then decided he would silence any possible witness against him, surely little or nothing would actually have happened. Almost certainly the Metropolitan police would have listened to Martin Standish's suspicions, looked at his father's notes, and then decided that whatever the truth about what had happened thirty years ago, there was not much they could do about it now. And the villain of the piece and his associates would have continued to get away scot-free. As it was, his ruthless attempt to shut everything down was precisely what had opened everything up. Surely Sophocles himself could not have imagined a more perfect irony?

The Old Bailey trial, as is frequent in cases involving fraud, was in Court 12 of what is generally referred to as "the new building." The public gallery was filled to capacity throughout the whole affair, and indeed there are few things the English appear to enjoy more than seeing the mighty humbled and the aristocracy reminded that the laws of England apply as much to them as to the rest of us. The media were full of it, while countless tweets and Facebook exchanges held forth on every conceivable aspect of the matter and one or two aspects that might have seemed *in*conceivable to any but the authors of the tweets. There were at least two op-eds in prominent newspapers pointing out that since the duke's heir was unmarried, already in his fifties, and hardly likely to find a suitable bride in the place where he was most probably going to spend the next ten or fifteen years, there was every reason to suppose that yet another of England's dwindling number of non-royal dukedoms was about to disappear. Whether you regarded this as good, bad, or of no interest whatever depended, of course, on your politics and your attitude to tradition.

The only real disappointment was perhaps that the duke and his heir pleaded guilty to all charges. So the trial did not take as long as do most trials involving fraud and there were none of those splendid court clashes and exchanges that might have been expected in a case of such magnitude involving persons of such stature. The fun, good though it was, was soon over.

At the end of it the duke was sentenced to thirty years in prison, and his son to fifteen.

When judgement was pronounced, the seventy-six year old duke was observed by some to look at the judge, whom he had occasionally met socially in his previous life, and say, "Oh, my lady, I shall never do it!"

The judge looked down on the old blackguard and shook her head.

"Never mind, George," she said quietly. "Just do what you can."

FORTY-THREE

Exeter, Heavitree Police Station.
The office of the Chief Superintendent.
Several weeks later.

I t was a cool, blustery day in early January when Chief Superintendent Davies summoned Cecilia to his office.

"I'm afraid," he said, "I have some very sad news. Ian Salmon
died in St Mary's Hospital in London last night. I gather he'd done
a full day's work at the National Crime Agency and had pretty
well sealed the nailing of a criminal gang that had been extorting
money from small businesses in Walthamstow for several months.
He was actually leaving to go home when he collapsed. They
rushed him to the St Mary's emergency room, but his condition
was terminal, and had been for some time. He died three hours
later."

"I'm so sorry," she said. "I'd really come to admire him. And
in a funny way, to like him very much."

Davies nodded.

"I know," he said. "Olwen was fond of him too — way back
from our days in the army. She's very upset." He sighed. "Ian was
a true public servant — in the proper sense. He cared nothing for

himself or his own rank or recognition. The *res pubblica* was what mattered to him. There aren't enough such people about. We shall miss him."

Cecilia nodded.

> *He was a man, take him for all in all,*
> *I shall not look upon his like again.*

Davies continued, "Ian has, by his own wish, already been buried privately. But there's to be a memorial service at St Martin-in-the-Fields on Saturday morning at eleven o'clock. In his last notes, scribbled in hospital while he was dying, he specifically says he would be honoured if all or any of those magnificent people from Exeter who worked with him on the case that involved the Haldon Hill murder could be present. Olwen and I will be leaving here at about half-past six on Saturday morning and driving up for the service, and we'd be very pleased if you and Michael could join us. We're also arranging cars for all the other members of your team who wish to come, and also for Bob Coulter and his fiancée."

"I'm sure Michael will want to come," she said. "I'll call him and confirm it as soon as we've finished talking."

"Good. Now I hate to seem crass, but life goes on and there are some other matters following from Ian's death that we have to deal with. I already knew he was very clear about the arrangements that he hoped would follow his death, and it seems the powers-that-be have pretty well fallen in with what he wanted. And they have moved very quickly. The first thing affects me personally, and I wanted to tell you myself, since you and I have worked together for some years — as I hope, happily: certainly so from my point of view."

Cecilia nodded, and waited, wondering what could be coming. Certainly her association with Glyn Davies had been a happy one as far as she was concerned.

"The thing is," he said, "I am to be Ian's replacement at the National Crime Agency — with effect from the first of February."

"Oh!"

This was not something she had either anticipated or desired.

"I mean," she said, "I'm pleased for you, but I'm sad for us."

"Thank you," he said, "though I think maybe it is time for me to move on. New challenges, and all that! Only last week Olwen was saying she thought I'd been getting too comfortable!"

He paused, and looked around his office, not, she thought, without some measure of regret at the prospect of leaving it.

"Anyway," he continued, "the point I'm coming to in my wordy Welsh way is this: my departure leaves this office vacant. I've been in conversation with the Chief Constable this morning, and he's already indicated his preferred replacement. It's you. Normally of course it would be someone from outside, but in this case he wants to make an exception. I personally hope very much that you'll accept the promotion and the job. As I'm here until the end of the month, that would give us a week or so for me to help you work into things, if you liked."

This too was the last thing she had expected and not at all what she wanted. She hardly knew what to say.

"Well," she stammered. "I never thought — I mean, I'm honoured — "

"It's not all honour," he said. "Frankly, it means a lot more politicking and committees and a lot less real police work. The reason the Chief Constable wants you to do it — and I agree with him — is that you're smart and sophisticated enough to handle the politics but you're a copper at heart. You won't lose sight of what it's about."

There was a pause.

"Who would lead Serious Crimes?" she said at last.

"If you're Chief Superintendent you'll have a major say in that."

"Verity Jones seems to me to be the obvious person. And not just because she's my friend."

He nodded.

"I dare say that seems obvious to a good many other people too. Verity's promotion is if anything overdue. But we'd need to deal with your promotion first, and then you could deal with hers and the others in order."

Another pause.

"Could I have a day or so to think about it? I'd like to talk to Michael."

"Of course."

Another pause.

"Oh — and there is one other thing," he said. "As Chief Super-intendent, I'm afraid you'll have to go back to wearing uniform most of the time while you're on duty. No more plain clothes elegance."

She laughed.

"Michael always says he fancies me in uniform anyway!"

EPILOGUE

Everyone who had been involved in the black ops murders investigation and all that followed from it attended the memorial service for Ian Salmon at St Martin-in-the-Fields in London. It was a quiet affair: dignified, simple, low key, and very much, Cecilia thought, in character with the man himself.

A young woman chorister sang William Blake's "And did those feet in ancient times" to Sir Hubert Parry's "Jerusalem." She sang beautifully, and her voice had a flawless, bell-like purity that one used at one time to associate exclusively with boy choristers. Certainly Blake's words were appropriate for Ian Salmon:

> *I will not cease from mental fight,*
> *Nor shall my sword sleep in my hand,*
> *Till we have built Jerusalem*
> *In England's green and pleasant land.*

Ian Salmon had been a very private person, and as various people spoke of him, Cecilia was surprised, as she suspected were others, to learn the breadth of his sympathies and the number of his charities. It was of a piece with everything else she knew of him that he made no parade of his faith, yet his chief reading over the last weeks of his life had, it transpired, been Jeremy Taylor's *Holy Living and Holy Dying*, of which there was a copy by his bed. He had faced death with quiet courage.

All this moved Cecilia very much. Yet she would always be clear what moved her most, what she would remember whenever she thought of that service in St Martin-in-the-Fields. It was the story Glyn Davies told of his last meeting with Ian Salmon.

"Ian," he said, "was up to his eyes in preparations for the summation of a particularly tricky case, and obviously very tired. Knowing his medical condition—he'd done me the honour of confiding in me some weeks earlier—I suggested he heed his doctors, who were constantly pointing out to him that he needed to conserve his energies, that if he rested more, he could expect to live longer. He gave that curious little half smile of his that I knew so well. And then he said, 'Glyn, I don't think that to neglect my duty can prolong my life in any worthwhile way.' That was the spirit in which Ian Salmon lived and died."

THE AUTHOR'S
ACKNOWLEDGEMENTS
AND THANKS

O nce again I must credit an episode of the wonderful BBC police series *New Tricks* for my starting idea for the story—a decades old black op that suddenly flares into dangerous life (*Part of a Whole*, Series 9, episode 10). As it happens, that episode was also the first time I saw a mobile telephone used as a listening device, although I have since seen the same and similar ideas several times elsewhere—notably in the American comedy thriller series *Leverage* and in *Burn Notice*. I love having my heroes (and villains) devise such things, since I am quite sure I would never be able to devise them myself! Of course and as always, no one but me is to be blamed for the use I've made of these ideas.

The friend of Michael Aarons who pointed out that even piracy requires collaboration was David Haskell, in his beautiful book, *The Forest Unseen: A Year's Watch in Nature* (Viking, Penguin, 2012). On page 6, with regard to the "entirely exploitative" horsehair worm he notes that, "even this parasitic worm is empowered by an interior crowd of mitochondria. Piracy is powered by collaboration."

When Cecilia was talking to Michael about Bob Coulter's red roses, the "song" she was quoting from was Pierangelo Bertoli's "*Rosso Colore*", which he released in 1974. The lines are:

Nella vita ogni cosa ha un suo colore,
e l'azzurro sta nel cielo, ed il verde sta nei prati,
ed il rosso è il colore dell'amore.

In life everything has its own colour,
and blue is in the sky, and green is in the meadows,
and red is the colour of love.

Incidentally, Bob Coulter (who is insatiably curious and as a result knows about a good many things you wouldn't expect him to know about) was perhaps more precisely aware what he was doing when he sent the red roses to Brenda than either Cecilia or Michael were aware. According to Mandy Kirkby's *A Victorian Flower Dictionary: The Language of Flowers Companion* (London: Macmillan, 2011) the crimson rose is "for a message of passionate love".

In conclusion, I must yet again say "thank you" to my many conversation partners, most of whom might by now be characterized in the immortal words of Captain Luis Renault as "the usual suspects" — first of course Wendy, who continues to put up with me; and then especially on this occasion Major R. M. Begbie, who on matters military cheerfully corrects my frequent blunders; and then also Renni Browne, Suzanne Dunstan, Chris Egan, Julia Gatta and Shannon Roberts. Thank you very much, all of you, for continuing to look at my pieces of trivia, to listen to my questions, and to point out my many mistakes, thereby indulging me in the enormous pleasure I get from writing these little stories.

Christopher Bryan,
All Saints, 2017.

ABOUT THE AUTHOR

Photograph by Wendy Bryan

Sometime Woodward Scholar of Wadham College, Oxford, Christopher Bryan is an Anglican priest, novelist, and academic. He and his wife Wendy live in Sewanee, Tennessee and Exeter, England. His earlier novels include *Siding Star* (Diamond Press, 2012), which was named to Kirkus Reviews Best Books of 2013, *Peacekeeper* (Diamond Press, 2013), *Singularity* (Diamond Press, 2014), *A Habit of Death* (Diamond Press, 2015) and *The Dogleg Murders* (Diamond Press, 2016). Author and critic Parker Bauer in *The Weekly Standard* Book Review describes them as "ideal antidotes to the crypto-farces of Dan Brown." Bryan's academic studies include *Listening to the Bible: The Art of Faithful Biblical Interpretation* (Oxford University Press, 2014), *The Resurrection of the Messiah* (Oxford University Press, 2011), the popular *And God Spoke* (Cowley, 2012) (which was among the books chosen as commended reading for the Bishops at the 2008 Lambeth Conference), and *Render to Caesar: Jesus, the Early Church, and the Roman Superpower* (Oxford University Press, 2005).

Sermon p.138

CPSIA information can be obtained
at www.ICGtesting.com
Printed in the USA
BVOW03s0244051217
501989BV00001B/42/P